This is a work of fiction
people, places, or eve
coincidental.
CALM BY THE CHRISTMAS TREE
First edition. November 1, 2020.
Copyright © 2020 Katie Burton
Written by Katie Burton
ISBN: 979-8-6964-2307-4

Calm By The Christmas Tree

Short Stories to Help Your Festive Spirit Soar

By

Katie Burton

This book is dedicated to:

Mum and Dad.

Thank you for everything you have done

and continue to do.

Contents

INTRODUCTION 9

1 – CHRISTMAS AT THE AIRPORT 11

2 - DRIVING HOME FOR CHRISTMAS 16

3 - THE SNOWMAN MURDERS 25

4 - ABIGAIL'S PARTY 32

5 - WORKING OVER CHRISTMAS 50

6 - SPENDING CHRISTMAS APART 54

7 – 'TWAS THE NIGHT BEFORE CHRISTMAS
72

8 - JAY'S CHRISTMAS CRISIS 82

9 - GIVING BACK AT CHRISTMAS 101

10 - THE CHRISTMAS BRIDE 118

11 – LONELY THIS CHRISTMAS	122
12 – NICOLE'S CHRISTMAS PRESENT	131
13 - DEAR SANTA	140
14 - THE MAGIC OF CHRISTMAS	145
EPILOGUE	163
ACKNOWLEDGMENTS	169
ABOUT THE AUTHOR	172

Introduction

December is a busy month, and often we forget to take time for ourselves during the craziness of the lead up to Christmas. With this collection of short stories and flash fiction, allow yourself to be transported to another world for five or ten minutes at a time. Give yourself permission to indulge in a little "me" time. Pour a tea or coffee, or whatever you may drink, and read me on the sofa beside the fire. Or read me on your daily commute to drop the kids at school or getting yourself to work.

One of the best parts about December is the build up to Christmas. Let your inner child be indulged, as you join me for 14 short stories and pieces of flash fiction in the lead up to one of the most wonderful times of the year.

"Christmas isn't a season;

It's a feeling"

- Edna Ferber

The characters and events portrayed in this book are fictitious. Any similarity to real persons, living or dead, is coincidental and not intended by the author.

No part of this book may be reproduced, stored in a retrieval system, or transmitted in any form or by any means; electronic, mechanical, photocopying, recording, or otherwise, without express written permission of the author and publisher.

1 – Christmas At The Airport

"Merry Christmas, have a good flight."

"Have a good flight, Merry Christmas."

"Yes, you too, have a healthy and safe one."

The cabin crew were ushering the final passengers onto the last plane before midnight, and a sudden calm fell over the deserted boarding area.

Adam looked around at the plastic glasses and chocolate wrappers littering the floor. A child's toy had managed to be left behind under a row of seats just a few steps away from the gate. He could imagine the meltdown there was going to be when the child discovered the toy missing. The amount of space in the normally busy departure lounge both scared and soothed him. He hadn't seen it this quiet since that first weekend of flights after lockdown lifted those years ago. It had been quite a while since he had worked Christmas Eve, and, if he was being honest, Adam was already trying to think who he could swap shifts with for next year.

Walking from the departure gate through to the shops and restaurants, Adam saw friends and colleagues hugging one another and wishing each other a good festive season. Some of them were now home for the week, getting to spend it with family. Adam, on the other hand, knew he would be working again in just a few hours, and was dreaming of his bed. He hadn't had to work the last few Christmases due to the age of his children, but it was only fair that he be given the Christmas shifts this year.

Shop after shop was closing up as he walked past, the shutters coming down, and final till drops taking place. Sales assistants were pulling on their coats while laughing and talking about their plans for Christmas dinner. The cleaner's cart was abandoned by a row of seats. As Adam got closer to the doors, his thoughts turned to the disruption and mayhem of the last few days.

Snow and ice had caused serious delays across the country, and the last plane before midnight had been one that was delayed by several hours. As usual, some passengers had been angry verging on abusive. Others had celebrated the chance to drink more and enjoy the tinny festive music being played over the speakers in the bar. One particular woman had become increasingly aggressive as the delay got longer and longer, and Adam had had to threaten her with calling security. In the end she had calmed down when offered a free food voucher. He had learnt long ago that sometimes the easiest way to deal with those people was to give them something, grovel, and then complain about them to his colleagues over a drink of coffee or something stronger. Tonight? Well, tonight Adam just wanted home. The grumpy woman wasn't going to ruin his festive spirit right before bed.

At home was his wife, their two daughters, three sons, and the rabbit. People always laughed when he included the rabbit, but it really was an important part of the family. Recently, Flopsy had seemed rather down and not her normal self. After multiple trips to the vet, lots of treats, and an abundance of attention from the children, Adam and his wife had decided there would be a surprise for everyone on Christmas Day when they went down to open their presents. He couldn't wait to see their faces when the children realised Flopsy had a friend who had moved in on Christmas Eve! However, they had been very careful to make sure there wouldn't be colony of rabbits by the time next Christmas rolled around.

With only a few people still working around the airport, and no passengers yet for the next flight in four hours, Adam walked into an empty car park. He threw his jacket onto the passenger seat, started the car, and began the journey home.

Each red light seemed to haunt him, and all he wanted was to sleep. But Adam held onto the image in his head of his five children on Christmas Day. Working extra shifts and rarely being at home would all be worth it when he saw their excited faces over presents in the morning.

Someone had once told him Christmas is for the children, but they were wrong Adam decided. No, Christmas is for the parents. To remind them of the magic and excitement of their youth, and to encourage them to relive that happiness as often as they could.

2 - Driving Home For Christmas

Chris Rea started on the radio, and James stabbed at the "off" button. Not helpful. He did i need that kind of music right now. Not when he was stressed and late and *Would the car in front like to find its accelerator?!*

The red lights from the cars in front could have looked somewhat festive, were he not in a foul mood. Having had a furious row with his wife the night before, James felt he needed to get home to fix things. His parents had always told him not to let arguments linger, especially over Christmas. You argue, but you fix it. You definitely did not start a new year with ill will.

It wasn't like he had planned to be working away over the Christmas period. His boss had announced at the beginning of December that someone would need to go to the London office over Christmas to be trained for the New Year. Essentially a promotion in all but name, and James had been the one selected to go. The training meant his salary would increase, he would be working fewer hours, and no longer would he run the risk of being asked to call into the office on a Saturday or Sunday to finish off the work that a superior couldn't be bothered doing. So why hadn't Vicky been happy for him?

The car in front trickled forward, and James debated whether he really wanted to take off the handbrake, drive forward about half a metre, and have to stop again. Or would he sit and wait for there to be more of a drive? However, the car behind made the decision for him when they blared the horn, startling him into stalling. Cursing under his breath, James restarted the engine to trickle forward half a car length. The M8 was manic tonight, but he was so close being home. In fact, if it hadn't been for this amount of traffic, he would've been at exit seventeen in a matter of minutes, and home again within another five or ten from there.

But Christmas traffic was always heavy, and Christmas Eve was the worst. Everyone was trying to get home, or into each other's houses to celebrate Christmas, and of course they had all had the same thought of *"It won't be that bad on Christmas Eve"*. How wrong they all were. It seemed every driver from Glasgow was on the road tonight, and James couldn't help but wish he had just stayed in London and ignored his parents' advice on arguments.

As he trickled round the next bend in the road, James spotted a pile up on the hard shoulder. Everyone rubbernecking to see it seemed to be the cause of the worst of the traffic, but up ahead the road looked clearer. Forty cars sat between him and the accident, which was being attended by the police and ambulance services, and then he would be on the home straight. He willed the car in front to just keep going.

The fight with Vicky replayed in his head as the traffic began to move a little faster.

*

"What do you mean you won't be home for the family dinner tomorrow?" she sighed with sheer exasperation down the phone. "You said you would. In fact, you *promised* you would. Your exact words were the London office is closed on Christmas Eve, Christmas Day, and Boxing Day, so you would travel up overnight on the twenty third, and back again on Boxing Day so that we would actually get to see each other for two whole days. Your parents are on their way here!"

"I know what I said, Vicks," James was getting irate now and pacing around his hotel room, focusing hard on not kicking the suitcase that lay half packed on the floor. "I'm not the director of the company. Nor am I the one who suddenly announced that everyone needed to work Christmas Eve and Boxing Day to catch up on the work that should have been finished a week ago! Do you really think I want to be stuck in this city?"

"Well I'm beginning to think that, yes," Vicky snapped down the line. James could almost see her sucking her teeth in anger. He didn't need to see her do it, he could hear it down the line.

"For God's sake, Vicky, I've already said I'm sorry! What more do you want from me? Do you want me to drive a nine hundred mile round trip on Christmas Day to get to you at two in the afternoon, to have to leave again at three just to make sure I make it home and can actually get some sleep before work the next day? We both know that's just not possible," unable to keep the anger out of his voice, James thumped the table beside him. "Just because you don't want your parents to know I'm not actually living at home at the minute, even if it's for work, all because you have some twisted imagination that makes you think they'll cut you off if your husband isn't living with you, that's not my fault. You know what? Forget it. I'll see you in the new year. I'll call you when I'm free."

"Don't bother. And don't bother coming home. Because if you're only doing it to make yourself look good, then I don't want to see you. God, you're such a child! All I wanted was to see my husband on Christmas Day for our first year as a married couple but right now I don't even want to think about you, let alone see you! Forget presents, for Christmas I want a divorce!"

The line went dead at that point, and James hurled his mobile across the room in frustration. She didn't mean it. She couldn't.

*

Driving at ten miles an hour towards exit sixteen, he glanced down at the shattered screen of his smartphone and regretted it even more. One of the big cracks went right down the middle of the screen, ironically splitting apart the lock screen photo of Vicky and him on their wedding day, smiling at the camera. He heard in his head again the advice his parents had given him the day before the wedding. Let Vicky do things she wants to do but be there to help her when it doesn't go to plan. Remember that marriage takes a lot of work to keep it going, but they should always want to do the work otherwise it's not worth it. And never leave a fight unresolved, especially over the holiday period.

"Come on...," James willed the car in front to drive. There was a gap now and if he could just squeeze through said gap he would be off the motorway. Looking at the clock, he had fifteen minutes in which to make it to the house to get to spend all of Christmas Day with his wife. He turned the radio back on and flicked it to play his Christmas CD. He needed something to lift his mood from all this traffic. James didn't want to be arriving home to Vicky in a bad mood when all he really wanted was to hold her tight and apologise for everything he had said and done over the last lot of weeks. The first song that came on was Driving Home For Christmas, and James forced himself to sing along to it. It was rather appropriate he supposed. When the song ended, Fairytale of New York began, and James found himself laughing and singing along as loudly as he could. The anger and resentment he felt towards the traffic around him was flung out into the car, and he felt lighter as he drove along the last stretch of the road. Scientists were right, singing really does make you feel better!

When James pulled up outside the house, he noticed the lights were all still on in the living room, and the clock changed to display midnight. Deciding to ignore the complaints he would get from their neighbours, James blasted the horn of the car until Vicky appeared at the window to see what the commotion was about. When she saw James standing at the bottom of the garden path, her face lit up and she disappeared from the window only to appear at the front door a few seconds later.

"Merry Christmas, Vicky!" James shouted as he ran towards her, bundling her into his arms and swinging her around in a circle as he leaned in to kiss her. She was laughing and crying as she kissed him back, and as he put her down, he asked her why the tears.

"Well I was going to phone you in the morning, but... I'm pregnant! Merry Christmas, James".

3 - The Snowman Murders

The first one had appeared on a Saturday night, or the early hours of Sunday morning, no one could be quite sure which, but it was overnight anyway. The snow had been falling heavily for a week by then, and it wasn't unusual to see snowmen pop up in the neighbourhood. No, what had been unusual was when the snowmen began to melt, and a child discovered the body of a woman hidden inside the snowman by the park. The poor woman was early twenties and had clearly been murdered.

As the days went on and the local police didn't seem to be getting any further with their investigations, people became suspicious of each other. Any time a new snowman appeared somewhere in the town, the adults would watch carefully. They asked their children who had built it. If a snowman stayed unclaimed for more than a few hours, panic set in. If one of the locals was missing from their usual routine, a search party was launched. Global warming had led to the town seeing particularly harsh winters, with the snow often lasting from November until mid-April. No one quite knew when the snow would thaw, nor did they want it to in case more bodies appeared. But many figured that when the snow stopped falling, no more bodies would appear.

*

Bodies two and three were found a week later, one on each side of town. The mayor was overheard in the pub claiming that if you stood on the steps of the town hall, looking towards the church, one body had been on the most easterly edge and the most westerly edge of the town. This time, the bodies of two young boys, their eyes open and unseeing from their blue faces. None of the bodies belonged to locals, but they also weren't on a missing persons database as far as the police could tell. Whispered theories began to mount as to who was leaving the corpses, why they were hidden in the snowmen, and when the next one would be discovered.

Another snowman appeared, this time at the gate to the cemetery, with a top hat and a cane. When none of the children of the town could identify who had built the snowman, the police put their crime scene tape around it before discovering the fourth body inside. This time a man, presumed to be in his sixties. Again, no record of him on any database, nor could they identify a cause of death.

So far, none of the victims could be linked. If there was a serial killer living amongst us, we were oblivious to who it was. Nor could anyone identify the bodies to help gain an idea where they had come from.

A week later, four more bodies were discovered, and the town announced a ban on building snowmen. People were afraid to leave their homes. Children no longer wanted to have snowball fights or go down the hills in the park on their sleighs. Adults could be seen putting heaters out, or turning the hose on the snow, trying anything they could think of to melt it quickly. No snow meant no snowmen, and no snowmen meant no more unexplained deaths. Soon they wouldn't trust the neighbours they had known all their lives.

*

The last snowman grave was found on Christmas Eve, exactly three weeks since the first body had been discovered. I'm the one who found it, stationed outside my back door beside the old coal bunker. Knowing immediately no child would've broken the rules and built one, especially not so close to someone's house, I phoned the police to report it. They were at the house within ten minutes, and I was driven to the station to give a statement. I was there for several hours, being asked about security cameras or footprints or any inexplicable noises from during the night. All I could say was the murderer clearly knew what they were doing, as the coal bunker wasn't covered by my security cameras. I hadn't heard or seen anything suspicious, and I certainly didn't come across any footprints in the snow around my back door. Once everything was clear, and there was no chance of me accidentally destroying any evidence possibly left by the murderer, I was allowed to return home.

As the police car approached the house, curtains began to twitch. I knew I would be the new topic of conversation women had over cups of tea or at the local shop, while the men in the pub would loudly proclaim whether or not they thought I had built the snowman myself to give them something to talk about.

I walked in through the back door, noticing the bare patch of ground where the snowman had stood merely hours before. Hanging up my coat, I flicked the switch on the kettle, and walked over to the chest freezer to lift out a frozen pizza for dinner. Pushing bags and boxes out of the way, I had to move the last three bodies out of the way to grab my pepperoni pizza.

As I turned on the oven and read the cooking instructions, I found myself wondering how to next dispose of the people currently taking up space in my freezer. I'd better think fast though. I had bought a turkey large enough for twelve people over Christmas, so would need room in the freezer for the leftovers.

Popping the pizza in the oven, I found myself wondering if there was a way to hide the last three bodies all in one big snowman the next town over. They'd never know what hit them...

4 - Abigail's Party

The scratching of pens and the clicking of laptop keys could be heard under the excited murmuring between friends. Dr Baldwin was droning on at the front of the lecture hall, but Abigail had stopped listening a good five minutes ago. Was he completely unaware that the rest of the room had too?

It was the last lecture the fourth year Psychology students had before they broke up for study leave, Christmas exams, and Christmas break itself. Already Abigail had packed away her notepad and pens; she had to rush back to the flat as soon as their lecturer finished talking. He was simply reminding them once again that the textbook he had co-written was compulsory reading and could be bought at the reasonable price of just £79.99 from the university bookshop. Unaware she was shaking her leg, Abigail felt her flat mate and best friend, Hazel, press her hand tightly down on Abigail's leg. She couldn't help it. Dr Baldwin had already overrun by five minutes and showed no intentions of stopping. Hazel, the perfect student, kept writing regardless of the time and her friend's obvious anxious energy. Abigail would simply have to get the notes from her at a later stage.

How could he still be talking?

"... And I must say that I am unimpressed by the noise levels in this room today. Given there are only twenty five of you in this lecture theatre, your whispering like a pack of school girls is as obvious to me as I am sure it is to the students who value what I have been saying," Dr Baldwin coughed haughtily and glanced around the room, pushing his rimless glasses up his face and scrunching his nose at the same time. Abigail found herself internally begging him to finish soon, promising things she would never say out loud, all in the hopes of him falling silent and allowing them to leave. She pulled her phone out of her pocket and started to text their flat group chat to ask someone to turn the oven on for her.

Today was their annual flat Christmas Dinner, and Abigail was the only chef. That was how it had always been, and she liked it that way. Knowing she couldn't miss her last lecture, Abigail had stayed up late the night before to prepare everything she could. Her schedule had been worked out into five-minute time slots, including how long she had to shower and change for the party later that night. It didn't help that their other flat mate, Natasha, had invited her boyfriend to their group meal at the last minute. There was just so much to do, and it felt like her lecturer was keeping them late on purpose.

"I suppose, many of you are eager for me to dismiss you. All I ask is another minute of your time...", Abigail's ears picked up the signs Dr Baldwin was finishing up, "... to wish you all good luck with your exams in the upcoming weeks, and to wish you a Merry Christmas and a Happy New Year. Remember to complete the *compulsory* reading over the break!"

Anything else their lecturer said was drowned out by the sound of chair seats flipping back into place as the students rose and called out festive greetings to each other from opposite ends of the hall.

Looking around her briefly and noticing Hazel's red head amongst a crowd of girls Abigail didn't know all that well, she lifted her bag and walked briskly back to their flat. Hazel's glance over her shoulder confirmed her suspicions that even today her socially awkward friend wouldn't stay behind to talk to the other students. Instead, Abigail was rushing home to prepare... At that moment, Hazel's stomach grumbled loudly in anticipation of their Christmas feast.

*

As she joined the throng of people leaving their classes and heading into the snow outside, Abigail tugged her coat closer around her body and shivered as the wind whistled in through the open door at the end of the corridor. Like many around her, Abigail started rummaging through her bag for her hat, scarf and gloves as they were all reminded that once again the warmth and security of autumn had given way to the sharp bite of winter. Only in Scotland would she still see people walking about in shorts and flipflops though, as she noted some idiot pushing past her. He was probably on his way to the gym or the students' union. Either way, Abigail was just grateful she had thought to bring her black beanie with her today as she pulled it down over her ears. With the top of her head protected, she wound her university scarf tightly around her neck to ward off the cold and keep the ends of her hair dry. If there was one thing Abigail did not have time for today, it was to restyle her hair before the party tonight.

Moving closer and closer to the fresh air outside, her mind ran through the first five steps she had to complete when she got in through the front door of her flat. The list was taped up outside the kitchen, on the living room door, and on her bedroom door, and yet Abigail had memorised that itinerary. Even two minutes spent reading the schedule for today's meal was two minutes too long as she really needed every possible second.

Finally making it out the door, Abigail could hear snippets of other peoples' conversations. Everyone seemed to be heading in the same direction, the Students' Union. If you could prove you had just left your last lecture of the semester, the union would give you two free pints 'to welcome in the holiday spirit'. Nothing said Christmas more than a room full of drunken students laughing and cajoling when they should've been studying for their exams. There were promises of mince pies, cocktail sausages, live Christmas music from the university's a cappella group, and so much more. In fact, that's where Abigails' flat mates and friends were heading to, while she walked on by to cook her favourite meal of the year.

"To start the mousse, grate 50g of chocolate and leave to one side. Melt the remaining chocolate in a bowl and stir in the orange liqueur. Whisk egg whites into stiff peaks and whisk in the sugar. Whip cream in a separate bowl…", Abigail muttered to herself as she crossed the university grounds and out into the main street amongst fellow students and the general public rushing about their busy lives.

Frozen leaves and branches snapped under her as her feet traced the familiar path back to the flat. After living in halls in first year, Abigail had moved with three friends to a small but comfortable flat just behind the university. The walk to and from the flat lead them along the treelined road that cars drove to access the staff carpark. At this time of year, it was certainly safer than trying to navigate the icy back lanes and alleys between the flats and the university. Even the refuge collectors were cautious about those pathways now that the frost had settled. As Abigail chuckled under her breath at the thought of one of them slipping on the ice and falling into a bin, her foot went from under her on a patch of black ice, causing her to laugh even harder. She hadn't hurt herself, and thankfully by now there was no one around to notice her embarrassing moment. Climbing back to her feet and promising herself that she would be more careful, Abigail let her mind wander back over the last few weeks and just how much work she had to do before her Christmas exams.

*

Slipping her key into the lock and walking in through the front door, Abigail was pleasantly surprised to hear her remaining flat mates' voices floating towards her from around the flat. The heating was on, causing her to start shedding layers the second she walked through the door, and once again Abigail found herself grateful for the contact lenses she was wearing instead of her glasses. Calling out her hellos, Abigail hung up her coat, slipped on her slippers, and tied her hair back on top of her head in a messy bun.

"What time are we eating?"

"Hello to you too, Ruari," Abigail laughed, being questioned the second she opened the door into the living room. "Can you not read the timetables I've dotted up all over the place?"

"Yeah, but I wasn't sure how right those times would be, or if there was any chance we could eat slightly later? I haven't even started drinking yet, and I need to catch up with the other engineering students in the pub first," Ruari sauntered out of the kitchen area, still in his pyjamas, a bowl of some chocolate based cereal in his hand, and his blonde hair doing its morning impression of Boris Johnston.

When they'd first met during fresher's week, Ruari and Abigail had immediately hit it off. Their shared interest in music meant they had spent many nights just sitting listening to whatever new album had been released that week, a bottle of wine or two between them, and they just talked until the early hours of the morning. With his messy blonde hair and dishevelled dress sense, Abigail felt he could easily have had a girlfriend if only he bothered to get out of bed and actually socialise with people. And here he was, all 6ft1 of him standing in her kitchen on the one day she insisted everyone leave her in peace.

"You know fine well I am not postponing this meal. My times have all been figured out for weeks now, and it's not my fault you skipped your nine-a.m. lecture so haven't started drinking yet. Now, if you would be so kind as to eat your cereal, wash your bowl, and leave my kitchen, I'd like to get started as soon as possible," Abigail sighed. Ruari had really wound her up today and she had only been in his company for a matter of minutes. What would she be like if he didn't leave soon? And what did he expect her to say? "Oh, and by the way, if you show up here too drunk to eat then I will personally sneak in in the middle of the night, shave your golden locks from your head, and cut all the strings on the guitar that sits so nicely on its stand beside the bed."

"Woah, what've you done to anger the beast, Ruari?" Natasha, their fourth flat mate, sauntered in and flopped down on the sofa, studying her nails intently. Standing by the table, Abigail could see Natasha's boyfriend, William, hovering in the doorway. He rolled his eyes, making Abigail stifle a laugh, before walking in and sitting on top of Natasha, much to her annoyance.

"He's being his usual self and getting in my way. Do you three not realise there is a strict schedule to follow today? I put it under all your doors and stuck it up in here, so you have no excuse for not knowing," Abigail whined. Why couldn't they just leave her to get on with it already?

"Come on Ruari, we'll get out of Abi's hair before she actually carries out one of her creative thoughts. She's read too many crime novels and seen too many tv shows for us to risk properly angering her," Natasha sprung up and dragged both William and Ruari out of the room, throwing a dazzling smile over her shoulder as her own honey-coloured hair swung in the loose waves she had clearly spent all morning perfecting.

Abigail had always admired her friend's ability to defuse a situation. Letting out a long sigh, she surveyed the mess of the kitchen and was very grateful that from half past eleven until twelve o'clock was a planned cleaning and tidying time. There was a lot to do before her friends returned to eat, and as she herself had said, there wasn't much time to waste! A quick dart of a tidy up should have the living room and kitchen ready for her to start on the mousse. As Abigail started to straighten the cushions on the sofas and gather the empty alcohol bottles from the floor, she began to question in her own mind whether the eggs for the mousse needed to be up to room temperature before she used them or not. It was going to be a long day!

*

As the clock struck five o'clock, Abigail served up her starter of pork terrine with a salad, and a small egg cup each of homemade cranberry sauce. Secret Santa presents had been exchanged, and the drinks had been flowing from lunchtime, so everyone was in high spirits. They all dived on the food in front of them, raising their glasses and wishing each other a Merry Christmas. Crackers were pulled, and before she knew it was happening Abigail found herself getting involved in the drinking games being played around the table without a care in the world about the rest of the cooking, or the party later that night. She was delighted with her Secret Santa present - a leather bound journal and an inkball pen for her to continue her poetry she loved to write. As was tradition, they were to try and guess throughout the night who had gifted which present, and Abigail was keeping it a secret that she had figured it all out a few weeks earlier. All those detective novels, along with her general interest in people, had led to her watching each of the others closely in the four weeks between drawing names and exchanging presents. That, and the others had asked her for advice on what to buy for each other.

"Before Abi returns to the kitchen to prepare the next part of dinner, I do believe it is Ruari's year to guess first!" Hazel shouted over the noise of her friends laughing and the Christmas playlist they had on in the background. When the others appeared to not have heard, she started tapping her knife against the side of her glass. Of course, no sound came other than the shattering of glass. It had the desired effect though, and everyone turned to look at what had happened. Whether it was the good mood, or the influence of alcohol, they all burst out laughing before trying to tidy up a little before the next course was served. By the time it was cleared up, Hazel had forgotten what she was even trying to say to them.

"Right. I'm about to go back into the kitchen but, before I go, I think Hazel's right. Ruari, who do you think bought your present this year?" Abigail leaned back in her chair, arms crossed, and took a sip of her wine. By now she was pretty sure this was bottle number two, but she couldn't really be sure.

"Hmm... Well... What did I get again?" Ruari turned the colour of his Christmas jumper as he realised he hadn't really looked at his presents. Abigail rolled her eyes, knowing all too well that Hazel had spent forever trying to think of the perfect present for Ruari. There had always been a suspicion that those two would get together at some stage, but while they lived together it certainly wasn't going to happen. "Oh yes! My new pyjamas, slippers and dressing gown! They're so soft! I'm going to take a stab in the dark and guess they're from Tasha. She's brilliant at getting me presents, so no one else could've picked this well!"

Abigail left the room before rolling her eyes. Clearly Ruari's brain had turned to slush, much like the snow outside their windows. No one was allowed to confirm or deny until everyone had had their turn at guessing. With her head inside the oven, she heard Natasha claim her Wreck This Journal book and bottle of whisky had to be from Abigail. Flopping back into her seat after turning the potatoes and topping up her wine glass, Abigail brought out their ever-trusted deck of cards. A space was cleared in the middle, and they played their version of Texas Hold 'Em. Instead of betting money, you bet a number of drinks. It worked much the same way as the poker game, an initial bet of 1 drink, followed by a second bet of 2. At this stage, you could either fold or continue to play if you felt your hand was good enough. The last two in the round went head to head to see who was to drink the loser's drinks. A quick and easy way to get drunk, and deadly on a night out, but this time Abigail didn't care.

They continued to play and eat until the clock struck nine o'clock, when the girls gradually made their excuses and went to touch up their makeup and try to sober up a bit for the walk to Jayne's flat for the end of classes party. Staring at herself in the mirror, Abigail was glad to say that tonight she did not look as plain as normal. She had taken the time to curl her hair, perfected her makeup, and was finally fitting back into the dress she had worn to her final year Christmas disco at school. Okay, it was probably a little shorter than she would normally wear, and it was a lot more skin-tight than she remembered it being, but for the first time in months, Abigail found herself smiling when she looked in the mirror. A pair of opaque tights, her black heeled boots, and a Christmas jumper over the top, Abigail was ready to go out and cut loose for the night. Now if only she could walk in a straight enough line to get to her front door...

5 - Working Over Christmas

The clock struck five, and Danny sighed with relief. Only three hours left until handover, and the latest patient to arrive seemed to be well on the way to recovery. Her last patient had arrived in from a new nightclub somewhere in the city centre. Who knew nightclubs even were open on Christmas Eve?

Danny always panicked patients coming in from the clubs would be drugs related, or worse given the current trend of knife crime in the capital, but this one had been a simple case of too much alcohol. Reports from the ambulance team who had delivered her to the hospital were that the patient had been sick before they arrived, so the likelihood of any alcohol being left in her stomach was very low. The girl had been wheeled into a bay, hooked up to some fluids, and would be given a talking to when she came around again about the dangers of binge drinking. A bit pointless at Christmas, but it was protocol. Danny knew herself that all that was getting her through the end of the nightshift was the thought of bed, Christmas Day with her son, and a bottle of wine in front of the TV when everything else was done.

Danny walked the corridors, checking up on the various patients under her care, and ran through the list of everything that would need to be done before she could sleep. Being on nightshift had always terrified her, but these shifts made more sense when it came to arranging for someone to look after her son.

If Danny could get away shortly after eight, then she could stop off at the local 24-hour shop for a few things, and still be home on time to watch Ethan open his Santa presents. There was then the cleaning to do and a bit of preparation for their Christmas dinner, and then, if she was lucky, she would be able sleep for a few hours while Ethan played with his new toys and visited her parents a few doors down from them.

Her parents always offered to look after Ethan when she was working, especially when she was on the nightshift, but Danny had promised herself that she wouldn't rely on anyone to help with raising her son. He was her responsibility, and she would never let him feel like he was being pushed off onto someone else. That just wasn't an option.

Finding an empty break room, Danny pushed a couple of the chairs together into a makeshift bed and closed her eyes. The seconds seemed to drag by in the silence. Feeling like she would never be able to sleep in that position, Danny resigned herself to just resting her eyes and her body for a few minutes. She knew she should have been using the time to finish some paperwork, but Danny was just exhausted.

Just as she felt herself beginning to doze off, Danny's pager came to life with a loud *beep beep beep beep!* and with that she bounced out of the chairs and towards the door. As she hastened down the corridor, Danny's mother's voice reminded her, "There's no rest for the wicked!".

The time? 7:02am. Not long now until she could be at home with her small but perfectly imperfect family.

6 - Spending Christmas Apart

Bodies crushed against us as Alex and I twisted and bounced to the rhythm of the latest Calvin Harris song blasting out of the speakers above our heads, the multicoloured lights illuminating our faces. Drinks were flowing, and my feet were aching. We had been out for a celebratory dinner; Alex's latest album had been yet another hit, with talks taking place about maybe performing at the next MTV Music Awards.

Alex had been the one to suggest we go out afterwards to the new club that had opened recently, and I could see why. Actors and actresses mingled with models, who were in turn trying to get the attention of the football players. It was a who's who of celebrities, I couldn't help but think, downing another Skittle Bomb and reaching for a shot from a passing waitress. The idea of bumping into a journalist or photographer was not at all appealing, but for now my attention was purely on Alex.

It wasn't fair to say we were out celebrating just Alex's news. My last series had been nominated for six different categories in the BAFTAs, and I was also now in talks with one of the biggest streaming companies in the world to direct one of my new shows. With the two of us both seeing our careers reaching new peaks, it was becoming more and more difficult to spend time together. Shaking my head, I decided not to think about the months ahead when I would be alone in our house; instead I would focus on the sheer joy on Alex's face when the song that started her career started blaring out in some weird club remix version.

"This is amazing! Why didn't I record it like this?" Alex's voice broke through the wall of noise into my ear. In response, I just laughed and signalled I was heading to the bar for another drink.

Clubbing wasn't really my scene, but it was an integral part of both my life and Alex's. Whether I was networking, promoting a new series, or trying to sweet talk others in the industry to get involved, I just couldn't seem to avoid these over-crowded thumping sweat boxes filled with alcohol and intoxicated people. Although I did have to admit that being on the VIP list for some of London's most exclusive clubs did have its perks. No queues, a bit more space on the dance floor, and bar service was often easy to get.

This, however, was not the case tonight. The four members of staff behind the bar all seemed to not see me standing there waving my money at them for attention. Considering giving up and moving back to the group without a drink in my hand, I glanced over my shoulder at the crowd behind me. The majority of my colleagues were there, dancing and grinding against various members of Alex's production team, none of them seeming to care that their working day was starting in a mere five hours.

"What're you having?" The bartender's voice broke through my thoughts about what we needed to do the next morning. He seemed to be talking to someone behind me, rather than me who had been standing queuing a lot longer than a lot of the people around me.

I shook myself, realising I was too drunk to even begin thinking about the day's schedule.

"Double vodka, orange, no ice thanks," a woman with auburn hair, slightly shorter than me, called back to the bartender, smiling at me as she did so. "And you? You've been waiting here longer, let me get you this."

"Rum and diet coke, please, with a dash of lime," I half shouted, not sure if I was directing it at the bartender, or the woman beside me.

While I didn't enjoy clubbing, Alex and I knew just about anyone who would be at these clubs between the two of us, and yet in front of me stood someone new. Maybe a new musician just breaking through? Was she one of the runners up on that new talent show Channel 5 were running in competition to The X Factor? I couldn't be sure but wasn't going to risk losing a chance to get a drink. Just because I had an early start didn't mean I had to stop drinking any time soon.

"Enjoy!"

"Thank you!" I tried calling after her, but soon the top of the woman's head had been swallowed by the crowd who were now going crazy to Mr Brightside by The Killers. I made my way back to the group, sliding back into my space and pulling Alex in for a kiss. If tonight was our last night out for a while, I was going to enjoy every single second of it.

*

The curtains weren't closed properly, and the streetlight was lighting up my pillow. That was the only explanation for why it was so bright. And that incessant beeping... Where was it coming from? It couldn't be...

"Hey Google, what's the time?" I managed to whisper to the Google Home Mini sitting on the bedside table. Already I didn't want to know the answer. The sound of cars on the street outside had more or less confirmed my worst thoughts.

"The time is 6:55am," came back the robotic response, as I groaned and pulled the pillow over my head. As if it wasn't bad enough that I had only gone to bed three hours ago, I had managed to sleep through my alarm. Great. Just what I needed today of all days.

Removing the pillow and tentatively opening my eyes, I saw that Alex's side of the bed had already been straightened. Fabulous. Alex was up and about and hadn't thought to wake me. Well, I guessed I'd have to get used to it again. Every time Alex went on tour, I struggled to adjust for the first couple of weeks. Sleeping late, not sleeping at all, spending far too much time at the gym, the signs varied, but my friends and colleagues could always pick up on them, even when they didn't know in advance that Alex was out of town.

"Coffee's on the table, and I've left you some painkillers here too!" Alex's voice came up through the floorboards. "You might want to add them to your shopping list for while I'm gone...".

The rest of the conversation disappeared as I rolled over and sent my head spinning.

Clothes were everywhere, like we'd undressed in a hurry and with no intention of ever again wearing them. I laughed to myself as I found one of my shoes under Alex's pillow, the other in the bathroom when I made it in there to wash the mascara smears off my face. It was still a little early to try turning on any lights. Makeup would have to wait a little while. Today was definitely a day for sunglasses and a high ponytail, there simply wasn't time to start washing and drying my hair.

"Is the coffee in a travel mug? Because that's the only way I'll have time for it at this rate!" I called over my shoulder, hearing Alex enter the room behind me. Tousled hair, a baggy white t-shirt tucked into the waistband of some black running shorts, and the trainers sticking out at the bottom, Alex was as breath-taking as ever, even in workout gear. I needed to stay focused. Where had my watch gone this time?

"Yep, already locked and loaded. Oh, and I made you a fruit salad to eat on your way too," Alex combed her wavy golden locks back and started to try and make sense of the bedroom. "You know, we really need to actually start putting clothes into the wardrobe after a night out. I can't find half of the stuff I'm meant to be packing, and I keep finding your clothes in my half of the wardrobe."

I scurried back into the bedroom, gathering the clothes from yesterday, and trying to find a simple skirt-suit for the day. Clearly not getting anywhere with these plans, I grabbed the navy dress Alex was waving at me and pulled it on over my head. Still no bra though. "See, one less dress in your wardrobe! Now if you could kindly magic away my headache, or at least go back in time and stop me from accepting drinks from strangers?"

It was at that point I spotted the bra lying on the floor at my side of the bed. One less thing to worry about. And the dress would just have to do. Dress off, bra on, dress back on again. Was that a stain on the dress? The dress came back off again immediately. This was not a good start to the day.

"Sorry, Chris, no can do on that one. But I can offer you a magical 15 minutes back in bed if you're destined to be late for work today?" That cheeky grin came out then and it was all I could do to refrain from rolling my eyes.

"And the rags think that I'm the bad influence on you? C'mon Alex, it's the first day of filming, I'm already running late, and as if that wasn't bad enough, this," I waved the dress around, "has a stain from who knows what. I'm a mess today!"

I ran down the stairs to the laundry room, shying away from the windows in case the neighbours caught a glimpse of me running around in my underwear like a lunatic. No clean office clothes, my hair looked like I'd been dragged through a bush backwards, and my girlfriend just wanted to spend the day in bed. Great. Why on the days when I don't have time does she always want to play coy?

In the laundry basket I found a pair of clean white jeans and a crisp denim shirt. A tad summery considering it's the middle of December... At that point I spotted Alex's mustard cable-knit jumper - perfect! Throwing my hair up into a messy bun, I grabbed my makeup bag from the sideboard in the hall and went on the hunt for shoes. Thankfully I'd been too lazy the night before to take out my earrings, they'd be fine for today.

"You can borrow my jumper if you'd like?" Alex appeared behind me, smirking and waving a pair of navy loafers over my shoulder. God she could be annoyingly smug when I overslept.

"It's something to remember you by while you're out galivanting. Where's the first stop again? Or have you taped the itinerary to the fridge?"

"Done you one better, it's saved to the calendar on your phone. And we're starting in Belfast this time. Which is why I asked if you'd like to come with us, even just for the first stop."

"You're a star," turning, I kissed her on the top of her head as I grabbed the shoes with one hand, and a scarf from the coat stand with the other. "What will I do without you for 6 months?"

"Probably the same as usual; get overly engrossed in work, listen to some of that sad music you love so much, phone me every chance you get, then moan about how messy I am when I get back!"

She did have a point - it would be nice to have the house to myself for a while. No one to judge me for listening to Westlife on repeat, or for leaving my clothes in little piles of outfits for the week ahead. Wait, did she say Belfast? I was half-way out the door when I realised she'd said Belfast. We could go visit the studios where Game of Thrones had been filming if I went.

"Okay. You're leaving tomorrow morning, with the first concert the following night, right? I can try and rearrange a couple of meetings? Maybe do video conferences or something. But only on the conditions we head to the Titanic Quarter, you don't bring me on stage in front of everyone at the concert, and I can fly home again the next morning. I need to be back in the studio on Friday, otherwise we'll be behind on filming, and we just don't have room in the budget for filming over the weekend," I bartered, pulling the door closed behind us before instantly regretting leaving the house without a coat. Alex nodded in agreement, sticking in her headphones to go for a run. She leaned in for a quick kiss goodbye, and then started off around the corner, and I just stood there shaking my head in disbelief. This girl could ask me to follow her into a burning building, and still I wouldn't be able to say no.

I turned and started walking in the other direction, towards the train station. Sipping on the coffee to keep me warm, I decided to buy a copy of The London Star on my way into work. The usual headlines of rumoured snowstorms due, politicians lying to their constituents, and... Wait. Why was there a picture of me in the bottom corner? Flicking quickly to page 27, I found a full article about the rumours that Alex and I were secretly engaged and would be announcing it at the end of Alex's world tour. Clearly the journalists knew something I didn't - our engagement was that secret even I didn't know about it! But at least it was just some harmless story.

As I folded the paper back up, deciding not to bother reading the rest, the train pulled into the station. For the first time today, something seemed to be going right. A woman settled into the seat beside me and asked if I was done with the paper. Nodding my consent to her taking it from me, I sat back to people watch as more commuters boarded the carriage.

*

Three stops later, I was rushing to get from one platform to another. If I missed the tube, I was definitely going to be late for work. Well, later than just ten minutes late. Making it just on time, I was too late to get a seat, and so committed myself to applying makeup standing up on the tube. This seemed to annoy the man in a suit standing opposite me, as he glared and rolled his eyes every time he caught me looking his way. It didn't matter to me, his opinion was his own, and for once I had managed to find a somewhat emptier carriage. There was actually enough room to set my bag on the ground and not accidentally elbow someone as I applied my mascara!

We slowed to a stop, and as I bent down to put the last of my makeup back into my bag in order to get off, the doors opened. Standing up quickly, I went to step forward as the businessman barged into me from behind, clearly in a hurry to get off. As I stumbled forwards, my lipstick managed to somehow bounce out of my hand, miss the gap between the tube and the platform, and landed at someone's feet. I followed the lipstick, and was just reaching down to grab it, when the other person also bent forward to retrieve it.

For a brief moment, I thought I recognised the woman who handed me back my lipstick. Her auburn hair and that smile... Where had I seen her before? But before I had time to think, she was stepping into the carriage I had just departed. I shouted a quick word of thanks over my shoulder and headed for the exit, her hazel eyes swimming in my mind as I tried to place her again. I shook myself from my thoughts and started the last few minutes of my walk to work. It was going to be a long day, and the woman was probably just an extra or someone I had seen every other morning without realising.

The glass doors opened automatically, and I swanned into the building, remembering a line Julie Andrews once used in a film; *"A Queen is never late, everyone else is simply early"*. Yes, that seemed about right. Security smiled and let me through without a second glance, and before long I was in my office and rearranging meetings for the next few days. Yes, I thought to myself, maybe a few days away is what I need. While I might not be an actual queen, I was the queen of the castle in my offices, and this queen wanted a few days away with her girlfriend.

Lifting the phone, I called my assistant. "Jo? Yeah, I'm needed across the water for a couple of days. Can we rearrange the meetings I have scheduled to either video calls or postpone them until next week? Thanks. Oh, and do me a favour and ask the script writers to come up here as soon as they can. Thanks!"

I sat back and began to mentally plan what I would pack, while reading the script left on my desk for filming on Friday. Maybe today wouldn't be so bad after all.

7 – 'Twas The Night Before Christmas

It was the night before Christmas. Sarah sat lonely in her apartment. It was the first time since she was fourteen that she found herself single at Christmas, and she didn't quite know what to do with herself. Scoffing at herself, Sarah realised that the last sixteen Christmas Eves had been spent either in bed with or messaging her significant other, and here she was after probably one of the worst years ever with absolutely no one to talk to. The only shows on the TV were either those religious documentaries, church services, or those cheesy romcom type Christmas films. Definitely not what Sarah was in the mood for! She could have flicked on Netflix, but not even Netflix and solo chill could fill more than five minutes for her.

Giving up, Sarah threw on a coat and hopped in her car, driving around on the lookout for something open. Most of the shops around her were closed, and the local church was ringing its bells to call all the parishioners in for their midnight service. Turning the corner opposite the library, Sarah found the one remaining pub in her town still open. Doors propped open to allow the crisp December air to circulate amongst the throbbing crowd, the sound of Mariah Carey being murdered by some woman on karaoke blasted around the neighbouring buildings.

Debating whether her need for company was stronger than her desire to be able to hear again, Sarah found herself parking up, crossing the road, and tucking her scarf up over her face. It wasn't all that long since they had had to stop wearing face coverings in busy public areas, and the reflex of covering her nose and mouth just came naturally now. There were still a few cars in the car park, probably those folk who had left on the promise of 'just the one drink then home', but the large crowd suggested the majority were locals who had been able to walk from their homes and would stagger home eventually, regretting their life decisions when the children woke at six the next day full of excitement at their Christmas presents.

Pushing through the crowd at the doors just to get inside the pub, Sarah overheard a group of men discussing how badly their football team was doing. As she got nearer the bar however, she noticed a woman sitting on her own, concentrating on her cup of what appeared to be coffee, and the crowd seemed to be leaving a bubble of space around her. Coffee on Christmas Eve? Sarah found herself silently praying there was alcohol of some kind in it to help numb the agony of listening to the five women huddled around the microphone belting out Mistletoe And Wine.

"This seat taken?" Sarah threw her coat down on the stool beside the mysterious woman, shooting her her friendliest smile as she did so.

"Be my guest," came the reply. The woman hadn't lifted her head, but Sarah could now see the e-reader in front of her and realised this might just be a mistake. People who bring books or e-readers to busy bars generally aren't looking for company. Sarah decided to have one drink, maybe perk up her Christmas spirit a little, then head home. She had a long drive to get to her parents' house in the morning. Drinking really wasn't the smartest idea.

As Sarah sat waiting to order, she allowed her eyes to take in the crowd around her. No matter how hard she tried not to, Sarah found herself gazing at the woman reading beside her. A little thinner than Sarah, but roughly the same age if she wasn't mistaken. Her chestnut locks were covering her face just enough that Sarah hadn't yet figured out what colour her eyes were. Deciding that, if it went horribly wrong, she could pretend to be drunk, Sarah tried starting up a conversation with this mystery woman thinking this would be the perfect way to pass the time.

"What're you having?" A young man behind the bar nodded at Sarah, wiping his hands on his black jeans. Probably trying to get rid of the excess beer that had just slopped over the side of the pint glass he had served to the elderly man sitting on his own at the other end of the bar. Sarah ordered a large glass of house red, before turning to the woman beside her.

"Would you like another coffee? I should probably have one myself, but then I wouldn't sleep at all. Worse than a child on Christmas Eve, I am!"

Silence.

Sarah shrugged at the bartender and paid for her wine when it appeared. Maybe the woman was just engrossed in her book and hadn't heard her.

Sarah tried a few more times to start a conversation. Or even just to get a response out of her, but all she got were one-word answers. Even talking about the snowstorm that had hit two days earlier, which always got a response especially from people travelling through the town on business, all Sarah heard was either yes or no.

Finally, giving up in desperation, Sarah downed the end of her glass and decided to hit the ladies room before driving back home. After entering the toilets, Sarah heard the door open behind her, and before she had a chance to enter a stall, a tall young blonde said, "I think you're striking out".

Turning around to ask her what she meant by that, Sarah was cut short by this stranger grabbing her and kissing her. It wasn't unpleasant, but Sarah pulled away as quickly as she politely could. While the kiss was non-consensual, Sarah had learnt the hard way that angering a drunk by rejecting them can result in an overnight stay in hospital and a black eye to contend with.

"That's what you wanted to do to that woman reading isn't it," she smiled at Sarah, blinking slowly and grinning like the cat who got the cream. Sarah politely tried to feign ignorance and walk away into one of the stalls, however the blonde woman grabbed her again, kissing her harder this time. Sarah decided manners were going out the window and started to push the woman off her when the bathroom door opened again.

"Excuse me!" The woman who had been reading at the bar tapped the blonde on the shoulder. "I think you'll find that this woman doesn't particularly like having your tongue forced into her mouth. Nor does she appear at all comfortable with your hand groping her crotch the way you were when I first walked in."

Sarah stood in bewilderment as the blonde shrugged, winked seductively at her, and then just left without another word.

"Th- thank you. I have no idea where that came from!" Sarah stammered, staring directly into the ice blue eyes of her saviour.

"Sometimes the younger ones don't understand that we just want to be with someone our own age. Am I right?" the woman laughed, handing Sarah a tissue to fix her smeared makeup. "I'm Beth, by the way. Sorry, I realised you had been talking to me after you left and hoped I would catch you before you left the pub."

"Sarah," she extended her hand to both shake Beth's and take the tissue. "I'm just glad you came in when you did! I wasn't expecting to be jumped by someone who looked about half my age, that's for sure."

"Unfortunately, it seems the younger crowd are a lot more relaxed about just kissing random women in bathrooms. Certainly not how it was done a few years back. I at least like a woman to know my name before I kiss her," Beth glanced at Sarah, holding eye contact slightly longer than that of someone just making polite conversation.

Sarah realised she was holding her breath as she leaned in towards Beth. "Well, now that I know your name..."

She kissed Beth gently at first, waiting to see how it was received. After a slight hesitation, Beth kissed her back, increasing the pressure ever so slightly.

Sarah was kissing Beth deeply, her tongue rolling on Beth's and licking the roof of her mouth while Beth slid her hand up into Sarah's hair. They seemed to continue for what felt like a lifetime, not coming up for air, until the sound of the bathroom door opening shocked them into stopping. They jumped apart as three teenagers giggled and hurried past them into the stalls.

Smiling coyly, Beth tucked a strand of Sarah's hair behind her ear and whispered, "Will we go back to yours?"

Leading her by the hand, Sarah walked them out of the toilets, through the crowded bar, and over to the car. She couldn't wait any longer. The drive back to her apartment seemed to take twice as long as the journey to the bar. They got in through the front door before they started kissing again. Bouncing from wall to wall along the corridor, Sarah lead the way into her bedroom and kicked the door shut behind them. This would be one Christmas Eve to go down in her memory forever.

8 - Jay's Christmas Crisis

Jay sipped at the vodka and orange juice, struggling back through the crowd to where Megan stood singing into her now empty glass. Megan was the one on the guest list for tonight. Something about her boss wanting an exclusive on whether or not Alex Starr and Christina Palladio would be engaged before Alex went off on a new world tour. Pulling a few strings, Megan had managed to get a plus one to bring Jay along, and then had proceeded to get that drunk Jay was having to play catch up.

"Guess who I just bought a drink for?" Jay shouted into her ear as the entire club began to belt out the chorus to Mr Brightside.

"I dunno, is one of the girls from Little Mix here? At least that would make some sort of story!" Megan was beginning to tire of trying to get close enough to her target couple to see rings on fingers. Their friends seemed to surround them and shield them from everyone else in the club.

"Nope. I'd make you guess again, but I'm tired and want my bed," Jay downed half the drink in one gulp, wincing. It wasn't fresh orange juice. Should've specified that. "While Palladio may have moved on from Skittle Bombs and shots to rum and Diet Coke, I can tell you for sure there is no sign of an engagement ring on that finger. Can we go home now? We could stop for chips on the way?"

Megan sighed, rolled her eyes, and nodded. It was time to go, and if Jay was right then there clearly wasn't an engagement story to share in their gossip column tomorrow.

Overjoyed at the fact they were escaping, Jay finished what was left in the glass, and danced out the door into the fresh air. While Jay had no problem whatsoever with working the nightshift in the shop, staying out all night while Megan worked was not Jay's idea of fun. Especially when Megan had got the job Jay had so desperately wanted when leaving university.

Checking that Megan was still following, Jay put an inch to her stride as she strutted towards the taxi rank around the corner from the club. You would think these cars would be waiting anxiously at the doors, hoping to pick up a celebrity who would give a generous tip. The crisp air of the December night was sobering, and Jay found herself wishing it was safer to walk home. A bit of air would do her the world of good. Then again, she thought, climbing into the back of a taxi, this would get her home in a matter of minutes, meaning less time listening to Megan whining about how unfair it was that she had wasted a night when her thoughts could have been focused on something a lot more important to the readers of The London Star.

As expected, Megan was only a few paces behind her, and clambered in through the other door. Jay watched out the window as the taxi moved off, spotting some poor WAG lying on the pavement beside a pile of sick. She could only assume this was yet another celeb from the club, who had managed to have either too much to drink or had decided that mixing alcohol with the latest diet pill was a great idea. At least there were people looking after the poor girl.

Arriving home, Jay went straight to bed, setting an alarm for eight o'clock so she wouldn't lose the whole day to sleep. She had an early shift tomorrow, and the idea of rushing into work and trying to avoid being late just did not appeal. Pulling the blankets up over her head, Jay realised she hadn't taken her make up off yet but decided it could just stay there. The lights were out, and it had been a long but uneventful night for the wanna-be journalist.

Tomorrow, Jay vowed. Tomorrow would be the day she would apply for a new job. Something that would actually make use of her degree. Her last thought before falling into a dreamless sleep was of the WAG lying on the freezing cold pavement, surrounded by strangers, and how at least she had a little bit of gossip for her blog.

*

Jay's alarm woke her the next morning, as it did most mornings. Did she know when she first woke up that Tuesday morning in December what the day would bring? No, but then do we ever fully know what a difference a day makes? As Jay threw her hand out from under the covers, the blast of cold air hit her newly exposed limbs, and Jay felt alive. She counted herself lucky to be able to see her breath in the air - something that had always amused her - even though she was inside her flat. Mental note made to fix the timer on the central heating, Jay grabbed a towel from the icy radiator and stumbled towards the bathroom she shared with Megan.

The flat seemed eerily quiet, but Jay just assumed Megan was sleeping off her hangover. That girl. The two of them may have gone to university together, and Megan may be one of Jay's closest friends, but she just could not handle her drink.

The boiler hissed as the shower sprung to life, and Jay rummaged around their cupboard looking for the spare toothpaste she knew was in there somewhere. Shampoos, conditioners, soap... Jay even managed to lay hands on a spare do it yourself home dye kit that must have survived the last Halloween party. Either that or the two girls had been drunk when they agreed to change Jay's hair from its auburn hue to a midnight blue. Whoops, the box somehow landed in the bin. If Megan wanted it, she could lift it out later.

Stepping into the shower, Jay caught a glimpse of herself in the mirror above the sink and cringed at the makeup smeared down her cheeks. Her body sighed with relief as the waterfall hit the top of her head, soaking her hair until it melted and moulded to the shape of her head.

As Jay started to massage in the shampoo, she felt like one of those actresses you see on the television ads, trying to tempt you into buying whatever latest new fad was on the market. Which reminded her, Jay needed to write up that review of the new shampoo and conditioner set she had been sent a month previously. With the illusion of bliss and sanctity shattered, and the day not getting any younger, Jay hurried to finish in the shower. It was too chilly a day to even consider letting her hair dry naturally, and so Jay sacrificed breakfast in favour of looking presentable.

Throwing things into a handbag, Jay came across a pile of CVs and remembered her resolve from only a few hours ago. Jay needed a new job. And so, the CVs were added into the mix of hairbrush, makeup, purse, breakfast bars, and whatever else might be rolling around the bottom of the bag. A tartan scarf to match her navy trench coat, and Jay was off out the door, ready to take on the new day.

This new-found optimism lasted a matter of seconds; a lorry driving through a puddle at the side of the road, just as Jay stepped forward to begin the walk to the tube. Absolutely drenched, she let loose a string of expletives a pirate would be embarrassed by and stormed down the road. Just what she needed today.

Along the route, Jay tried to read the *'We're Hiring!'* notices hung in shop windows, and managed to find enough change in her pocket to buy three different newspapers in the hopes of finding time and space on the commute to search within their rustling folds for an exciting new opportunity. Blogging and moonlighting as a sales assistant in a shop wasn't exactly the job Jay had dreamed about as a little girl.

*

Jay's mind took her back to a conversation with another girl from her course. Sarah always wanted to know why, if Jay was an established blogger, would she ever want a job in proper journalism? Back then Jay had been resolute. Blogging was a hobby. Being a journalist was all she had ever dreamt of. The hustle and bustle of a busy office, people buying a print copy of what you had to say on a daily basis, it just made so much more sense. Plus, Jay had argued, there's always room for new journalists on the block. How wrong had she been?

Leaving university 3 years earlier, Jay hadn't had a single interview. Nor had any of her impromptu applications been successful. At that stage, Jay threw herself back into blogging; improving her stats, working on building a loyal reading base, and prioritising quality over quantity of posts. It filled a void created by the lack of a position in the journalism industry, but blogging was no longer cutting it as a full-time profession. In fact, as Jay walked along the platform towards where the doors would always stop, she realised she hadn't posted in quite a while. Maybe it wasn't blogging that wasn't right for her, but rather the entire industry in general?

Shaking this idea from her head, Jay shuffled towards the yellow line as the carriage pulled into the platform.

"*Smile, Jay*," she thought to herself. "*There are worse things in life than having a quarter life crisis while standing in a train station.*"

The doors opened, and as they did so a lipstick seemed to bounce out of the carriage directly towards Jay. It came to a rest just in front of her foot, and as she reached forward to pick it up, another hand reached towards it. Picking up that small black tube, Jay smiled at the woman to whom it belonged and handed it across. Their eyes met briefly, and Jay felt a jolt of recognition.

Christina Palladio, the director Megan and she had been tailing just last night, was the owner of the hand receiving the lipstick. Christina's smile of thanks didn't quite reach her emerald eyes, a confusion behind them as if she recognised Jay but wasn't entirely sure where from. Without giving her the chance to remember, Jay pushed past and onto the carriage Christina had just vacated, and, as the doors closed, she disappeared into the crowd of Londoners heading about their morning commute.

Jay found herself somewhat wound up by the lack of recognition. Okay, yes, the club had been dark, and she could only imagine the number of drinks that had been consumed, but a stranger buys you a drink at a bar and you don't even recognise them five hours later? The life of someone higher up the food chain Jay supposed. Exhaling heavily, she pulled paper number one out of her bag and began to browse the job listings as quickly as possible.

*

By the time Jay made it into the shop and clocked in, the tiny digital clock on the till registered 9:02am. She was quite proud of the fact she had made it into work only an hour after waking up! The shop floor was empty, with only one man standing at the magazines opposite. As he took his time choosing between three different TV guides, Jay managed to secretly slide her phone onto the counter and begin the job hunt on it. Plenty of opportunities to work from home or join one of those pyramid schemes - no thank you.

It was time to stop being picky and just look at any job she was officially qualified for regardless of whether or not she actually wanted to do it. Not everyone wants to work in a shop all day every day, but there are others who would've given their left arm to have Jay's position in this shop, so it was only fair that she move on and let them have the chance. At that point, Jay decided she was going to slip a copy of her CV into the middle of any businessperson's shopping. In fact, the shop was in the middle of handing out leaflets with every receipt, detailing what offers they had going on in store, alongside local updates on what events were taking place in the local community centre. Sure, the majority of them would end up in the bin, but it was better than just standing here all day wishing her life away.

After ten o'clock, it began to pick up the pace again. More and more customers were coming in to do bigger shops, and Jay's CV found its way into shopping bags, handbags, even into a baby's pram at one stage. It became a game to see how imaginative she could be in finding ways to send someone out the door with a copy.

Just as Jay was trying to surreptitiously slide a copy in between two magazines, the woman who's shopping she was packing laughed, "Well I suppose that's one way to further the job hunt! Is there anything in particular you're looking to do?"

At first, Jay was mortified at having been caught. Like a rabbit in the headlights, Jay stumbled over her words. "Oh... Um... Well, you see, I... Well I suppose no, I'm no longer being fussy. You can read it for yourself, I'm a qualified journalist, just currently trying to find someone who'll hire me as a writer."

She didn't know why, but there was something about the young woman in front of her that made Jay want to tell her all her secrets. The woman looked tired. Not in the way of someone who has had a restless night, but more like someone who had been on the treadmill of life for months, maybe years, without stopping. As if stopping would mean admitting defeat. The bags under her eyes had been covered in concealer, but not well enough to actually hide them. And she wasn't one of those "new mum" types that you see in the shop around this time, no that was a different kind of tired. Here was a woman who seemed to be at least thirty years older on the inside than the outside, as if she had experienced more life than any of the rest of us.

"Well then I hope someone manages to pull you out of the retail sector, if that's what you're hoping for. Although, if you're ever interested in joining those of us in healthcare," her tired brown eyes had darted down to the purse in her hands, "give me a call and we'll see what we can do about getting you in even on a voluntary basis to begin with."

The strange woman handed Jay a business card that simply read:

Dr. D. Blake
Email - d.blake@setrust.hscengland.net
Phone - 020 7946 0558

Doctor. Great, here Jay was judging someone for looking exhausted, and knowing her luck this doctor would be the one pumping her stomach the next time she drank too much too quickly at some boring party.

"Thanks, I will," Jay pocketed the card so as not to appear rude. There was no way she would be getting involved in the healthcare sector, but she didn't need to hurt this kind woman. It takes a certain kind of person to work in the NHS, and unfortunately Jay was not that kind of person.

Dr Blake paid for her shopping and left the shop without another word spoken between them. However, Jay did find she no longer wanted to subject strangers to receiving a copy of her CV. The doctor had made her think about what it was she really wanted to do. And suddenly Jay had gone full circle in the matter of a few hours. Maybe this business just wasn't for her. But if it wasn't the right path, then what was?

*

The journey home from Jay's shift at three o'clock was nowhere near as eventful or exciting as the morning commute, if you could even call the morning commute eventful. Jay had lost all motivation to hand out her CV, instead now wondering if perhaps she needed to lie in bed eating ice cream from the tub, watching feel good films, and moaning to Megan about how unfair life was.

"Megan had better be in the mood for Bridget Jones' Diary," Jay thought to herself, turning her key in the lock. It was exactly the film she needed today. A woman who wanted to break into publishing accidentally getting a job in television all because she slept with the boss. Unfortunately for Jay, sleeping with her current boss would probably just result in a trip to the STD clinic, and even more time to mope

around the flat. Speaking of, the flat was still cold, and there was no sign of Megan having left for work this morning as her keys were still in the bowl by the door. Not taking a second thought about it, Jay headed for the kitchen to make up some lunch, presuming Megan had decided to work from home for the day in order to nurse her hangover.

A culinary masterpiece was needed - one consisting of carbs, carbs and more carbs. A crisp sandwich would be the excellent cure for Megan's hangover, and it would certainly give Jay something new to hate about herself rather than just be annoyed at her lack of direction in life.

Jay plated the two sandwiches, added a chocolate bar to each plate, and balanced a bottle of water under her arm as she sauntered down the corridor to Megan's room. If she was still in bed, then she could stay there and keep Jay company as she tried to figure out where she was going with her life. Pushing the door open with her bum, Jay backed into the room and set the plates down with a crash. Megan didn't move from under the covers, so Jay walked to the opposite side of the bed to get in beside her and wake her up with her cold feet against her legs.

Except when Jay got around to the other side of the bed, Megan was staring straight through her with unseeing eyes. A pile of vomit beside her on the bed, and a blue tinge to her lips. Jay froze, unsure what to do. Gingerly reaching forward, Jay went to shake her shoulder just in case it was all an act. But Megan's skin was as cold as the snow that had fallen from the sky last week.

All thoughts of food long forgotten, Jay scrambled back out of the room and down the hall to their phone. She dialled 999 and, as calmly as possible, told the person on the other end of the phone that she had just discovered her friend dead in her bed. And only a week until Christmas.

9 - Giving Back At Christmas

Arya sat watching the Christmas shoppers bustling down the busy high street from her corner office window. She never understood the concept of over-spending at Christmas. Nor did she understand pretending to be a great person for one day of the year. What made people think this was the most wonderful time of the year? Pavements were packed, shops were crammed, and all around her were signs of insincerity and commercialism. Grabbing her coat Arya prepared to leave for the day.

"Hey Arya. Any plans for Christmas Day? Are you getting to see your family?" John was throwing his coat over his shoulders, his snowman tie getting caught somehow up under the collar of the coat.

"Oh, hey John. No, nothing special planned. To be honest, I'll probably just sit at home, watch TV and have a microwave dinner," Arya felt she had to stop and talk. John was one of the only people in the office who didn't throw her sympathetic glances or whisper behind her back.

"Well Carol insisted I remind you, you're more than welcome at ours. Even if you just want to pop round for drinks or something, we run an open-door policy during the festive period!"

"Thanks, John, I appreciate it more then you know but I think I might just wallow in self-pity this year if you don't mind. Maybe at the New Year or something, yeah?" Arya saw the smile slip from John's face momentarily. Of course he hadn't forgotten. That's why he was asking. It wasn't just her husband killed by a drunk driver in the early hours of New Year's Day, John had lost a close friend. She suddenly felt guilty for even mentioning it.

Recovering his smile, John gave her a peck on the cheek as they moved outside and said, "Of course, I just thought... Well, New Year is more than okay, and I'll even come pick you up. You'll stay the night and I won't hear any arguments. I wish you would change your mind about Christmas though. Carol thinks of you like a sister, and we both hate the idea of you spending the holidays alone."

"Thanks. Tell Carol I was asking after her, and I'll definitely be there to see in the New Year. Anything will be better than the one we've just come through!"

John and Carol owned the company Arya worked for. She had worked there for almost seven years, and there were just 8 of them working in the office. Over time, Arya had grown close to her boss and his wife, and in turn they treated her like family. Both having come from small families themselves, John and Carol had asked Arya and Connel to be godparents and honorary relatives to their children. Having not been able to have children of their own, Arya and Connel had treated her boss's kids like their own, and likewise John and Carol were more like siblings than friends.

Stepping into the busy street, Arya braced herself against the onslaught of cold air, before turning to John and saying, "Have a good Christmas John, I'll see you a week on Monday. Enjoy your time off work and tell the kids to be good or Aunty Arya will tell Santa to leave them coal!"

"You too Arya. If you change your mind about Christmas Day, dinner will be around three o'clock. Come early if you like. See the kids opening their presents. But if we don't see you, have a good holiday and enjoy your time off as well. I'll come get you around six on New Year's Eve."

Arya walked into the car park and started to scrape the ice off the windscreen. She needed to stop at the supermarket and was dreading it. She knew she should have stopped earlier in the week, but work had been busy and all she had wanted to do was get home. Now of course she would pay for that decision. Shopping this close to Christmas was stupid. Families everywhere, kids crying they weren't allowed more sweets, adults bickering over which wine would go best with their starter... It really was not worth it this late on a Friday night.

Pulling into the car park at the local supermarket, Arya cursed out loud. Finding a spot was going to take some time. Driving around in circles for a solid twenty minutes, she finally spotted a car starting to back out. Pulling into the parking spot, Arya turned the car off and mentally ran through what she needed to get. Christmas Dinner always consisted of turkey breast, stuffing, mashed carrot and parsnip, and her favourite bottle of Malbec. Luckily for her, she could do one stop shopping and get home as quickly as possible.

Pushing the trolley, Arya grabbed what she needed and headed towards the checkout. Every queue was huge, and it looked like the store had turned off the self -service lanes. Arya thanked her lucky stars she had decided to buy less than ten items, but even that had a long wait of about thirty people in front of her. She had no choice but to stand in line and wait.

Glancing around, she saw all sorts of people and purchases. Some with trolleys piled high of food and presents, others with just a few items of this or that. The man in front truly had less than twenty items. Scanning his cart with her eyes, Arya saw milk, apples, cereal, kitchen roll, a tin of carrots and peas, stuffing and a single chicken breast. Smiling at the kid in the trolley in front of him, Arya noticed the child was holding onto a cuddly dog teddy for dear life. Chuckling to herself, Arya thought about herself at that age. The one toy she had owned as a child growing up was a small cloth doll that she took everywhere with her. One day however, Arya had managed to leave it at home and when she came home, the doll's head was torn off and one of its legs was burned half-way up, having somehow got too close to the fire.

The child's family were now at the register. Grabbing the little plastic divider, Arya put her stuff on the belt behind the man's and waited her turn. She watched as the woman with the child looked nervously from her purse to the till each time an item was scanned through.

"That will be thirty pounds and twelve pence, please. Cash or card?"

Watching the mother count out the money in her purse, Arya felt herself burning with embarrassment for the woman. Before she had met Connel, that had been her.

"Umm, how much?" The mother asked, even though the total was right there in front of her.

Somewhat impatiently the sales assistant repeated, "Thirty pounds and twelve pence."

"Uh, ok. Right. I'll have to leave something. I'll leave something..." the mother tailed off, rummaging through the shopping bag, keeping her head as low as possible to avoid eye contact. The man in front of Arya started tutting loudly.

"Would you like me to cancel the sale for you? You could come back with your credit card later," the sales assistant asked somewhat rudely.

"No, no don't do that. I can't come back later, we needed this. I'll..." The lady replied, her voice cracking as she angrily wiped away a tear that had dared to appear on her cheek.

"Well ok, how much do you have?"

"Twenty pounds and ninety pence. I can leave her nappies," she nodded at the child in the trolley. "We can make do, I'm sure we'll have something somewhere I can use instead."

"Jesus, could you hurry up? Some of us have places to go!" a sudden outburst from the man between Arya and the woman startled them all.

The lady at the till was now truly in tears. Trying to compose herself, she pulled the nappies out of the carrier bag.

Arya, however, had seen and heard enough. She stood there for a moment. As a general rule of life, she did not get into the middle of things. Her childhood was one where, no matter what the issue was, you kept quiet before someone made you.

"Oh sorry, I forgot we agreed I would put this through with my shopping this week and you would get the next one!" Arya smiled at the woman ahead, stepping around the man and his trolley. "You darted off in such a rush, I completely forgot. Sorry, can you just put those back into the bag for my friend?"

Smiling knowingly, the sales assistant handed the nappies back to the mother, and started bagging the rest of the items that he had already rung up.

"Please, you don't have to pay for my shopping," she whispered as Arya loaded the filled bags into the trolley.

"Honestly, I want to help. I know what it's like to be in your position, and just wish someone had been able to afford to help me out. Call it an early Christmas present."

The mother thanked her over and over again as she wheeled the trolley away, wiping at her face to remove the tears that continued to fall, as the child in the trolley babbled away happily oblivious to what had just been going on around her.

Arya watched as the woman headed toward the door and turned back to the cashier. "What a crazy night, huh?"

"You're not kidding. The holidays bring out the best and the worst in people. I'll just store her shop on the till until I finish with this customer...", the sales assistant glared at the man who had been so rude a few minutes earlier. He was finished up quickly, and Arya moved to the top of the queue.

"Some people wouldn't know the true meaning of Christmas spirit if it came up to them and bit them," Arya grumbled. She still was shaking with rage that the woman had been embarrassed in front of all these strangers.

"It's the time of year. Some become Scrooges, but very few remind us of the charity of the Christmas story. That'll be sixty pounds and seven pence."

Handing her card over, Arya moved her bags from the bagging area to her trolley and finished up paying before she rushed out of the store. Starting her car, Arya sighed to herself and forced away the memories that came bubbling up of helping in the homeless shelter with Connel last Christmas.

Charity had felt low down on her list of priorities recently, but helping out that family? It felt nice to help pay for the woman's items. Like maybe Christmas could be the same while still being different. Reversing out of her space, Arya headed for the exit. At least someone had had the sense to operate a one-way system for entering and leaving the car park! Just as she was about to turn towards home, Arya noticed the mother and toddler huddled together walking down along the footpath in the snow. Seeing neither of them had a coat on, never mind hats or gloves, Arya hesitated. Making a last-minute decision, she stuck her indicator on and pulled up beside them.

"Hey, let me give you a ride home," Arya called out the window into the wind. Even those few seconds of the bitter wind was enough to make her eyes water.

The woman looked bewildered as she replied, "Thank you, but we're okay to walk! It's only half a mile up the road but thank you. You've already helped so much tonight!"

"No, no, don't be daft. It's far too cold and windy for you two to walk home." Hopping out and running around to the pavement, Arya yanked the back door open wide. "Come on, I'll crank the heating up and hopefully we'll get you two warmed up a bit before you get home."

Consenting, the woman tentatively climbed into the back seat and put her child on her lap. "Thank you so much. Really though, we would've been fine walking."

Putting the car into gear, Arya waved off the thank you and got directions to their apartment. It was a lot further out than just half a mile, but she didn't feel that she could or should point that out. Pulling up to the building she was told to, she noticed the little girl was asleep.

"Well it seems you need some help. Let me carry the bags and you can carry her," Arya grabbed the bags from the back seat while the woman unlocked her front door and lead her up the three flights of stairs to the top floor.

Unlocking the door, the woman flicked the switch on the wall. Arya could sense her embarrassment as she stepped aside to set her child down and let Arya in. Stepping over to the counter, she set the bags down.

"Thank you so much. What's your name? You've done so much for me and I don't even know who you are. My name is Leanne, and this is Maisie," She said looking down at the little one.

"I'm Arya and really it was no problem. Why don't you go tuck her into her bed, and I'll get these out of the bags?"

Standing in the middle of the kitchen waiting for Leanne to return, Arya looked around. The apartment was pretty bare, a small sofa, end table, T.V and stand adorned the living room, with a small table-top tree decorated in paper chains and homemade decorations. A few children's toys dotted around the floor, but not many and they were obviously loved before.

Without waiting for Leanne to come back, Arya quietly let herself out and drove back to the supermarket. She headed straight for the toy aisle, and then continued to follow the twisty windy way of following every aisle around the shop until her trolley was full and too heavy to push. Arya joined the queues again, now slightly less busy than before, paid, and drove straight back to Leanne's building.

She had forgotten the door locked as she left. Realising she didn't have much option, Arya started unloading her shopping onto the front step. When done, she quickly scribbled a message into a card, and pressed the buzzer for the flat at the top of the three flights of stairs. Disguising her voice as best as she could, Arya heard herself tell Leanne to come down as there was a delivery for her, and then Arya ran back to the car to move before she was recognised.

Parking a few doors down, Arya watched in her rear-view mirror as Leanne opened the door to find the Christmas tree, decorations, toys, and every

Christmas themed food item Arya had been able to find in the shop. She watched as Leanne read the card, and didn't feel at all guilty when she saw that Leanne had a few tears falling down her face.

Driving home, Arya thought back over her note.

Leanne and Maisie,

Thank you both for reminding me. You've given me a gift no money could buy. A gift of memories of Christmases past, and a reminder that future ones can be good too. I hope you don't mind. I couldn't think of any other way to say thank you. Enjoy Christmas with each other, and I hope you have many more to come.

Wishing you the best for the holiday season,

Arya xx

While giving back at Christmas didn't always have to involve materialistic items or spending money,

Arya hope that Leanne and Maisie would appreciate the sentiment with which it was given. Time with loved ones is precious, and Arya just hoped the two would have many more years together.

Arya tapped at the dashboard of her car and loaded up the phone options. It rang three times before it was answered.

"Hello? Arya? Everything okay?"

"Hi, John, yeah all's good, sorry I just realised you're probably in the middle of your dinner, " Arya called out to the speaker phone as she turned another corner. "I was just wondering if that invite for Christmas was still open, and if you'd mind me staying for a couple of nights?"

10 - The Christmas Bride

"Robbie, wait!" She called out to him. He turned and watched as she ran to him, her white dress billowing and her hair flowing behind her.

"You married him," he mumbled, trying not to look up. If he looked up, she would see the tears that were blinding him.

"I didn't think you were coming back," she whispered, her voice loaded with love and despair, and all the hurt she had gone through over the last few months while he was missing, presumed dead.

"But you didn't know," Robbie looked up then to meet her eyes, seeing hers too were filled with tears.

"A bride can't cry on her wedding day," he whispered, gently stroking her cheek.

"It's my party and I'll cry if I want to," she quipped, half laughing as she choked back a sob. "I tried to wait for you, Robbie, I swear I did..."

Her words were cut off as he pulled her into a tight embrace. It was a hug that said everything and nothing. Neither of them spoke, yet with that hug they said everything they had wanted to say over the last few months. They said how much they missed each other. How much each needed the other. That hug was a symbol of their friendship and also their love.

Yet it also said Robbie knew she was no longer his. It showed her he respected her choices in marrying another man. A hug that said he would always love her, but now that love would have to change from romantic to platonic. She was still the love of his life, someone he could not live without, but he must now learn to. With their hug, he told her how much it pained him to see her marry someone else. He told her he had done everything he could to make it back before it was too late. That he needed to be the one to tell her he was alive.

Robbie understood her hug. It was her apology. Her love. Her thanks that he even showed up at her wedding, knowing the hurt it would cause him. It was her way of thanking him for letting her know himself that he was alive. She was apologising for giving up hope. For not waiting longer. For trying to move on when she knew deep down inside that she could never love another as much as she loved him.

The hug lasted mere seconds but felt like a lifetime. They each caught glimpses in their minds of what their life could have been. Today could have been their wedding. It should've been his family inside, celebrating the love this young couple shared. They saw their children playing in the back garden. A house they had picked out and decorated together. Visions of a dog bouncing between them all, as their cat lay lazily watching the world go by in the afternoon sun. Between them, they saw themselves growing old together, caring for one another in their old age. Images of a life that could've been but wasn't. It couldn't be now. She had chosen someone else.

As Robbie began to pull away, he whispered, "Merry Christmas, Helen. I hope you have a lifetime of happiness."

Helen watched as he turned away from her and walked down the drive, knowing this would be the last time she saw him. It was a mistake. Getting married on Christmas Eve was a mistake. They should've waited until Boxing Day.

11 – Lonely This Christmas

Henry hadn't always hated Christmas; there had been a point in his life when he had eagerly anticipated the season of giving and thankfulness. However, that had been back when he had a family around him and a reason to be grateful. Now all the festive spirit did was cause him more pain. As Henry shuffled through the stores and saw the decorations both on sale and decorating the town, they took him back to a time when his home was full of joy.

Every Christmas Eve had been the same. There would be the smell of orange, apple, cinnamon and cloves wafting through the house when he came home from work. He was greeted at the door by his young children running up to hug him, babbling excitedly about what they had done that day. Going into the kitchen, he would find his wife wearing her

Santa hat and a red apron, having just finished baking mince pies with the children to leave out for Santa. It was Henry's favourite memory of his wife, and it was the memory his mind turned to whenever they argued in the latter years. It always made him smile, thinking of his family at his favourite time of the year. In those latter years, the memory made him remember that whatever they were arguing about was a small thing compared to the love they all had for each other.

That was all gone now. Henry still had the house, and it was still decorated for Christmas. He had promised her it always would be. There was a tree in the corner, decorated with baubles and lights and the decorations their children had made all those years ago. Underneath the tree were the presents, as expected and directed. The garland was strung up and down the staircase, and across the front of the fireplace where the stockings were hung.

However, there was no fire lit. That had always been the rule on Christmas Eve. The children wouldn't let them light the fire in case Santa burnt himself on the dying embers, and so the tradition had stuck.

Even tonight, as Henry sat looking around and shivering against the cold, he refused to light the fire on the off chance even one of the children arrived at the door unexpectedly. Sitting in his favourite chair, Henry looked up at the painting hanging on the wall above the fireplace. They had had it commissioned on their twenty-fifth wedding anniversary; a portrait of his wife holding their newly born twin daughters, while Henry stood smiling down at their two sons. He used to tease his wife about her half smile that she wore in the portrait. Usually when she smiled, she had done it with her whole face. Her mouth would be wide open, teeth flashing, and her eyes would sparkle with joy. But she had always hated how her smile looked in pictures so she would wear that half smile when she knew a photo was being taken. She might have hated her smile, but Henry had loved it. He had loved her, all of her. He still loved her, even now after all this time had passed.

It was five years ago today that she had been taken from him. The house had been decorated, the cookies baked, and the presents wrapped and sitting under the tree, exactly as it was as Henry looked around him. He had been out at the park with his grandchildren, when a neighbour phoned him to say he needed to get to the hospital as quickly as possible. Henry remembered calmly hanging up the phone, loading the children into the car, and driving to the hospital, all before he realised he didn't know what had happened or who was in the hospital.

When Henry got to the hospital, he found out what they had refused to tell him on the phone. His wife, the love of his life, his childhood sweetheart, the person he pledged to love forever, was dead. No husband should have to identify the shattered remains of his wife.

The accident was a freak one. A bus driver had a stroke whilst driving and had died behind the wheel of his bus. Henry's wife had been walking down the footpath, having just delivered some freshly baked cookies to their neighbour a few doors down who was having her grandchildren over for afternoon tea. Witnesses said that when his wife saw the out of control bus, she had shouted for the children having a snowball fight a few metres away from her to move out of the way before diving behind a parked car herself. Except she was too late, and the bus had crushed her between the parked car, and the wall of the neighbour's garden.

Everyone was apologetic. The bus company paid him enough of a settlement to pay off a few of the children's debts and put enough aside that each grandchild would comfortably survive university. Friends and family tried for the first year or two to help him get past her death. At first their children had taken it in turns to stay with him, a new one each day calling in to bring by food or company in the way of grandchildren. They wanted him to take down the decorations and try to go on living.

Eventually they gave up. They had stopped calling in with him two years ago now, but the youngest daughter still phoned every two weeks. Henry only left the house now when he had to, and he avoided speaking to anyone as much as possible. He instead stayed home in his decorated house day after day and waited to be reunited with the love of his life.

*

It was Christmas Eve, and time for Henry's annual routine. He checked the children's rooms. He could almost see them sleeping peacefully in their beds. Henry and his wife had always made them go to bed early on Christmas Eve with the promise that Santa didn't visit children who stayed awake all night. He then checked to make sure the presents were piled up nicely, just in case any of his children and their families were able to visit him in the morning. Henry couldn't begin to imagine the trouble he would be in with his wife if the grandchildren came around and there were no presents for them. He then ate all but one of the cookies sitting out next to the "Thank You for the cookies" note from Santa, all before drinking the glass of milk and going to bed.

His wife came to him in his dreams every year on Christmas Eve. She cried and begged him to let her go, to start living again. She told him that it hurt her to watch him suffer. Henry held her in his arms and wiped away her tears. He thanked her for being his wife, and for making his life complete. For being the best mother and grandmother in the world. Henry held her and whispered that he would never let her go, that his love for her would never die. It was the one night of the year that he actually slept peacefully, with a smile on face.

*

Christmas Day dawned, and Henry woke to an empty house once again. He walked around it, opening curtains and imagining the families he saw on the street outside were coming to visit him. But they never were. Making himself a cup of tea, Henry sat in his armchair to drink it as he stared at the presents so meticulously wrapped and waiting. It had now been six weeks since he had last spoken to any of his children, and the hopes of them visiting were fading. Turning on the radio, Henry kept himself busy working on a jigsaw puzzle to take his mind off his wife, his children, and the passing of time.

When the clock struck four, he put a microwaveable roast dinner in to heat and poured himself a glass of wine. By five o'clock, he had eaten his Christmas dinner, washed the dishes, and was ready to fall asleep in front of the television. As he closed his eyes and drifted off to sleep, he glimpsed an illusion of his wife, standing in the kitchen doorway and smiling at him. It might not be the Christmas Day she would've wanted for him, but Henry didn't mind. He knew his children were busy with their families. He had never wanted to burden them, and so was okay with being left alone. Henry drifted off to sleep, dreaming of the day he would be reunited with his wife; a day he would no longer feel so alone in the world.

12 – Nicole's Christmas Present

Nicole took a sip from her mug of hot chocolate, the velvety sweetness trickling over her tongue and down her throat, as the snow fell outside. The silence of the forest around her home always made her yearn for her childhood. She hadn't always lived in a log cottage in the middle of nowhere, her only neighbours the wildlife around them.

Nicole's husband had asked her to move up north with him when they first met. He was set to take over his family's business, and her own family had all either died or lost touch. It had been the most sensible thing to do. After a few months of dating and getting to know each other, Nicole had said goodbye to her job in the day care centre and moved north with her husband. They were married within the year.

It had been a small affair, with just his family and some of the employees from the business. A winter wedding, unsurprisingly, and so Nicole had arrived at the church in a one-horse open sleigh - exactly the way she had always dreamt she would. The church had been decorated with white and blue flowers, and their colour scheme was blues and silvers. After the ceremony, they had their reception in a clearing in the forest. Festive drinks, soups, and a Christmas dinner were served to the small gathering of guests, and their first dance had been to Coldplay's Christmas Lights. It sounded crass, and Nicole was very glad none of her friends from her hometown had been able to travel up on time for the wedding, otherwise she would never have heard the end of it.

Moving away from the window, she threw another log on the fire. Her husband would be cold and tired when he got home, but she wanted to stay awake until he got back. His father had finally handed over the reins in June, and the last few months had been very busy. There was still so much to learn it seemed, and he never had time to just sit at home with her. Instead, all their time was spent in the business. Whether they were supervising the manufacturing process, testing out some of the new products, or checking the delivery addresses, the only time they ever got to spend together was at work. Nicole had come up with a plan.

Her plan was to wait up for him coming in from work. They'd agreed to exchange their presents on Christmas Day night, when they had both had time to relax and enjoy their meal. This year, Nicole was giving her husband the present of a holiday – a proper one where he wouldn't have to think about work, and they could relax by the sea in the heat. Nicole longed to feel the warm summer sun heating her closed eyelids as she lounged listening to the waves lapping at the sand. There was to be absolutely no talk of work or Christmas or anything to do with the family business.

The clock on the mantlepiece struck twelve, and Nicole was getting restless. Another five hours until her husband came home. Nicole decided to take a walk through the forest to kill some time. Pulling on her heavily padded coat and stuffing her feet into the snow boots lying by the door, Nicole braced herself for the icy blast as she stepped over the threshold and into the wild outdoors.

The snow falling muffled all sounds until all she could hear were her boots crunching through the previously undisturbed snow, her breath coming in short pants and sending out a cloud of mist in front of her with every step. Around her, birds lay in their nests, squirrels ran up and down trees, and Nicole once again reminded herself she would never have experienced this beauty if she had continued to live in the city.

Up ahead was a clearing, and Nicole's aim was to get there in order to watch the stars overhead. Her husband had taken the time to teach her everything he knew about them, including how to navigate purely by watching the positions of the stars. If she made it to the clearing, she could lie in the snow and watch the stars until it was time to meet her husband back at the house. As Nicole took a step into the clearing, her foot snapped a branch, the noise as loud as a gunshot in the silence of the night. Looking across the clearing, Nicole spotted some wild deer who were watching her in return. They appeared to decide she wasn't a threat when they turned and continued to strip the bark off a nearby tree.

Lying down in the middle of the clearing, Nicole stared at the stars and wondered how different they would look while lying on a beach. Having lived so close to the top of the world for so long, she was looking forward to taking her husband on an island hop around the different continents, staying as close to the Equator as she possibly could. Someone long ago had told her if you want to catch the winter sun, you need to travel to the southern hemisphere. However, Nicole was no longer sure she could cope with the tropical heats of South Africa in January, and so was happy to settle for the Greek or Spanish Islands she had dreamt about as a younger woman.

Yes. This year was the year Santa was going on a proper summer holiday in the middle of winter. Nicole had never really understood how much work went into preparing presents for every child in the world until she met Nick. His father, Nicholas, had tried to explain it to her before he retired, but she had never anticipated how attached Nick would become to every little aspect of the job. No doll could be sent without him checking the face had been painted on just right. No toy car would be delivered without a test drive first to make sure the wheels didn't come off over a certain speed. Nicole felt guilty every time she caught herself resenting the children for the care and attention her husband showed them, but she had known what she was getting herself into from the start. Not many first dates lead with them telling you their father is Santa Claus, and that in a little under ten years he is expected to replace him!

This year Nicole had arranged they would go on holiday. The elves in the workshop were under strict instructions to not start the production of any new toys for the following Christmas until the first day in January; the day Nicole planned on them returning. It of course meant they could only have a five-day holiday, leaving on Boxing Day, but it was still a much-needed rest for the pair of them.

As she had expected, Nicole lost track of time, and, before long, her eyes spotted what looked like a shooting star moving across the sky. At least, to anyone else it would look like a shooting star. Nicole's trained eyes knew the difference now between such a star and her husband's sleigh, and so she picked herself up off the ground and made her way back to the cabin to change into dry clothes. She got home and changed and had just finished heating the milk for some fresh hot chocolates, when she felt his arms around her waist.

Melting into him, Nicole whispered, "Merry Christmas, Santa."

"Merry Christmas, Mrs Claus," he murmured into her neck, leaning on her shoulders to support himself after a busy night. "How would you feel about us taking a little holiday?"

"Funny, I was just thinking the exact same thing," Nicole sighed with relief before turning and kissing her husband.

13 - Dear Santa

Dear Santa,

I hope you and Mrs Claus are well! I have been thinking about you and the reindeer a lot over the last lot of months. I haven't been so good, but you probably know that already. Every year I write to you and ask for some presents for Christmas, but Mummy says that might be difficult this year.

She says some of your elves went on strike, and that you found it hard to make all the toys for all the girls and boys. I asked her if you would still be able to bring me the fancy new bike I want to ask you for and she started to cry? I don't really know why.

Mummy says you see everything. That's how you know who belongs on the Naughty List and who goes on the Nice List. I think you'll have seen everything that happened here this year. You'll have seen all the times Daddy had Aunty Joan around at the house and told me to be a good boy and watch TV. And I'm almost definite I saw you the day he gave me a whole five-pound note for not telling Mummy Aunty Joan had had a nap with Daddy up in their bed. Why do adults have a nap in the afternoon? I thought only babies did that. But Daddy says adults need naps too, and they sometimes nap together to keep away the bad dreams. It didn't seem to work though, because Aunty Joan definitely was moaning in her sleep. I didn't go up to check on them, but I think she was having a bad dream.

Did you see how high I jumped on the trampoline you brought last year? I love it so much – it's my favourite present ever! Thank you so much! This year I would really love a new bike. My old one was taken from the garage in the middle of the night, and now I can't play with the big boys in my street. They go too fast on their big boy bikes for me to keep up when I'm just running behind them. Last week they were away for a full thirty minutes before they came back to find me! They said they didn't know I wasn't with them anymore. So pretty please can I have a super-fast bike so I can keep up with them?

If a bike is too hard to make this year, I would really like a new remote-control car. Mine was left in the old house – the one Daddy now lives in with Aunty Joan and her little girl. Mummy won't let me go play with her and gets really upset when I ask to go see and see him. Now if I want to see Daddy, another lady sits in the room while we play together. Mummy and Daddy argue all the time now, and Mummy said that's why we now live with Granny. But I'm not allowed to ask any questions.

The last thing I would like to ask you for this Christmas, Santa, is something you and the elves won't be able to make. But I want to ask, just in case you can do it since you are magic. The one thing I really really really want for Christmas is for Mummy and Daddy and me to all live together in one house again just the three of us, where no one shouts, and no one cries, and we go on holiday together to the beach. I know when the little girl in the film asked you for the big house, a Daddy and a baby brother you managed to do it, so I really hope you can do the same for me! But Mummy says that's just a film and stuff like that doesn't happen in real life. But you're Santa. You can do anything!

I will leave your cookies and milk by the Christmas tree this year. Granny doesn't have a fireplace, so she says you'll know to come in through the front door. I've made sure, and they won't lock it tonight so you can just walk in. Apparently, you have a magic key to let you in, but I've told them anyway to leave it open just in case. Rudolph and the other reindeer will have their usual carrots, and I can't wait to stay awake to see if I can hear you on the roof!

Hopefully hear you soon!

Love Peter, aged 8.

14 - The Magic of Christmas

The Christmas tree was lopsided, with a few bald spots, and even looked more pathetic with the few presents under it. However, it was all their father could afford. Ever since the divorce, he barely had enough money to pay bills, let alone buy presents for his children. Their mother had announced the day after Halloween that she couldn't live there anymore. That her family were suffocating her, and she needed to be free to breathe. So, while the divorce wasn't yet finalised, the separation had been hard on those left behind, and any festive spirit that might have filled the rooms with laughter had died down.

When their mother had left, their dad had to take a job working as a receptionist for a local financial service. It didn't pay a lot and meant that he worked long hours. It paid the rent and the bills and left them a little bit over at the end to buy them food to get by on. He didn't have enough to buy extras, so Simon decided to help by taking a job at a local department store. The hours were the same as Ben's school time, so their dad wouldn't have to pay for childcare. It only paid minimum wage, but Simon felt that he was doing his part to ease the financial pain of being a single father on minimum wage with a teenage son and one still in primary school. Between the two salaries, Simon and his father had been able to buy a few presents for Christmas so that Ben would at least still experience some of the magic Christmas was meant to bring to children of his age.

The two workers knew the true meaning of Christmas, and also knew there was no Santa Claus. They wanted to make sure Ben still believed in the magic of Christmas, especially now that Halloween would always be a reminder of the fact his mother had chosen to leave him.

Most nights, Simon would hear his dad crying and knew it was because he was lonely. One morning, when Ben was still upstairs getting ready for school, he asked him if he wouldn't consider getting back into the dating scene. He just bowed his head and admitted that while it sounded like a great idea, dating required money and energy that he just no longer seemed to have. Simon didn't push the subject but wished there was something he could do to help his dad. He prayed that some-day his dad would have the energy and confidence to get back out there.

*

It was Christmas Eve. They sent Ben to bed early and then got out the presents and placed them under the tree. Afterwards their Dad and Simon stood there hugging each other. He turned to Simon with tears in his eyes and whispered, "Merry Christmas, son."

Simon held back the tears and replied, "Thanks, Dad, but I don't feel like celebrating

Christmas this year, and there is no magic in Christmas for me. I will pretend for Ben's sake, but I couldn't care less if we just pretended tomorrow was the same day as any other."

The dad turned to him and frowned, "Now don't let what you mother did ruin your holiday spirit. There's always magic in the air at Christmas, you might just have to look harder to see it this year."

Simon grumbled, scowling at his dad and his mention of magic, "Bah hum-bug, good-night, Dad. I'll see you in the morning."

Simon walked upstairs into his room, got ready for bed, and tried to convince himself to just go to sleep. He had recently started taking part in online surveys and other competitions to try and save some more money. However, he had drawn the line at gambling. Not only was he underage, but he felt that it was a slippery slope, and just another way to lose money rather than make it.

He wasn't asleep for more than two hours when he heard a strange noise. Not sure what it or who it was, Simon found himself shaking with nerves as he crept out of bed. Picking up his baseball bat, trying to look courageous, Simon quietly walked towards the sound of the noise. Convinced someone was trying to steal the few presents they had managed to scrape together, Simon was definite he would stop at nothing to deter the burglar.

When he got near the living room where the lopsided tree was, Simon gasped, no one was there. The tree was loaded with presents and whoever had left them had left the front door open. Simon walked into the room and called out, "Who's there? What's going on? DAD!"

His dad came running as if he'd been hurt. When he entered the room, he stopped, grabbed the nearest chair to hold onto so he wouldn't fall over out of shock, and breathed, "Oh my goodness... Did you see? What?"

He blinked, rubbed his eyes, and said, "Am I dreaming?"

Simon walked over to him, put his arm around his dad and chirped, "No I don't think this is a dream." He pointed to tree and said, "I heard a noise and came running in here, and that is what I saw. Dad, how? Who... who could have done this?"

He just smiled and whispered, "All I can think of is the magic of Christmas... But between you and me, if Ben asks, it was Santa Claus, okay?"

Simon scratched his head, and mumbled "Okay, I'll pretend for his sake, but I still don't believe in the magic of Christmas. It was probably Mum with a guilty conscious or something." His dad just laughed and said, "Who knows, I've seen stranger miracles happen. As for your mum, that would be a stretch. Not unless she met a billionaire in the last few weeks!"

They hugged each other and his dad whispered, "Let's go back to bed before we wake

Ben. Simon, I want you to try and look surprised in the morning okay?"

They snuck back towards their bedrooms, checking on Ben to make sure he was still asleep. Giving his dad the thumbs up signal, Simon closed the door to his room and crawled back into bed.

He lay there unable to sleep with a million thoughts running through his head. He frowned to himself. By a process of elimination, he knew it definitely couldn't have been Santa Claus. Santa wasn't real. It could have been someone else, but he couldn't think of anyone who would do something as generous as that. It was then he began to consider what his dad had said, and found himself asking the darkness of his bedroom, "Is there really such a thing as the magic of Christmas?"

Suddenly, the darkness of his bedroom replied with a strange man's voice, "What makes you think there's not Christmas magic?"

Simon bolt upright in his bed, pulling the duvet up over his chest and squinting into the corners of the room in an attempt to glimpse the owner of the voice.

"Who's there?", he whispered, coughing to try and bring some depth back into his voice.

Whoever it had been never answered him though, and so he got out of bed to turn on the lights. No one was there. Simon decided he must have been dreaming, or at least imagined it, and so curled up under his blanket and eventually fell asleep.

Simon must have eventually dozed off again, because suddenly he heard the voice again, this time it said, "Christmas *is* magic, Simon."

Simon opened his eyes marginally and peered through half closed lids at the end of his bed. At the end of the bed, sat a jolly looking fat man with white hair and a red suit. It couldn't be... could it? Simon rubbed his eyes and stammered, "How... How did... How do you know my name?"

With a twinkle in his deep blue eyes, the man in the red suit replied, "I know everyone's name. Just like every child knows mine, albeit it changes depending on the country. If you believe, many things that seem impossible can happen this time of year."

All Simon could do was sit up and stumble over his words. His tongue felt like someone had glued it to the roof of his mouth. Words and sentences weren't even forming inside his head, never mind trying to actually vocalise his thoughts. "But... I don't.... "

The man moved closer and sat next to him, gently patted his shoulder, and said, "Simon, I know that you and your father have worked very hard to make Christmas happen for Ben. He's still trying to forget the hurt of this year. So, I'm giving you all something to make this Christmas extra special."

Simon finally found his tongue, and before he realised what he was doing he had shoved this man who appeared to imply he was some form of Santa

Claus off the bed. He turned towards him, spitting vehemently, "Why are you talking to me then? If Dad and Ben are so special, why are you talking to me?"

He just smiled at Simon in returned before sighing calmly, "You're the one who didn't believe in Christmas magic. I also know there was nothing under the tree for you, so I'm here to give it to you personally."

Simon looked at him with wide eyed amazement and cautiously said, "That's because I didn't want anything this year, except to make Ben happy."

Santa sat down on the bed again, waiting to see if Simon would push him away like he did last time. When he realised Simon was going to let him stay, he put his arm around the teenager and pulled him close.

"I know that's not true. I know you want your mum to come home. Or for the hurt and anger you feel towards her to go away. You just want someone to say 'I love you. I will never hurt you'. Let someone in, Simon. Let love and people who care about you in, and you'll experience the true magic of Christmas."

As the man in the red suit spoke, Simon felt what he could only describe as love radiate to the deepest part of his soul, where his injured spirit dwelled. Slowly, Simon began to relax and felt like the weight of the world that he had been carrying on his shoulders for the last few months was finally lifted. It was then he felt the Magic of Christmas surge through his body. Simon didn't know how the man did it, but he felt a peace come over him that he never felt before.

It was then Simon asked Santa, "Is this a dream, or am I talking in my sleep? You know, I do that sometimes, I wouldn't want my dad to hear me. He'd think I've lost my mind."

Santa laughed and his belly shook like a bowl full of jelly as he chuckled, "No, this is not a dream and you're not imaging things. We are sitting in your room, on your bed, and talking. You're the only one who can hear this conversation. Your dad and Ben will sleep soundly until the sun comes up in the morning."

His last words to Simon were, "Remember the magic."

*

The next thing Simon knew was Ben bouncing on his bed and singing that it was Christmas and that Santa had been. Ben was tugging at his arm and shouting, "Simooooooon, wake up! Santa's been here, you've got to see all the presents under the tree! There's like a bajillion for each of us!"

Simon sat up in bed, rubbed his eyes, and told himself, 'It was only a dream, there is no Santa Claus.'

He then looked at Ben, rolled his eyes and groaned, "I'm up! I'm awake… Give me a sec… Ben quit pulling on my arm, will you? You're hurting!"

As Ben ran out of the room, Simon grabbed his robe, put on his slippers and shuffled out of his room towards the living room and the Christmas tree. As he passed his dad's room, he saw Ben tugging on his arm too, trying to get him to hurry and go look at the tree. Simon entered the room, while his dad followed with Ben pulling him by the hand. Ben then jumped up and down clapping his hands, shrieking, "I told you there's a Santa Claus! I told you! I told you, didn't I?"

When Simon looked over at the tree, he gasped. It was no longer a scraggly old lopsided tree with just a few presents under it. Instead, it was a full beautiful tree with more lights and ornaments than Simon had ever seen before. It was then he felt his dad grab his arm. When he looked at his dad, he had a confused look about him and tears were forming in the corners of his eyes. Simon hugged him close and whispered, "There is true magic in the air at Christmas!"

Neither of them said anything else as they headed towards the tree to open their presents. When the last item was unwrapped and Ben was playing with his new toys, Simon and his dad headed toward the kitchen to make up some breakfast.

As Simon gathered the dishes to set the table, his dad headed for the fridge. Simon heard his dad shout in surprise, and when he looked the door was open wide and his dad had jumped back. Rushing over to see what had shocked his father, Simon looked inside the open fridge and saw more food than he had ever seen in their fridge before. There was a big ham, an even larger turkey, milk, fruit, vegetables, eggs, bacon, and all sorts of Christmas treats that he had only ever dreamt of buying this year.

Again, Simon wondered if Santa had been the one to bring all this stuff too, but quickly brushed the thought from his mind - it was Christmas, and anything could happen. It was then they heard someone knock on the front door.

Their dad went to answer it, and all Simon could hear was someone talking to him, but he couldn't tell if it was a male or female at the door. After a few minutes, he came back into the room beaming from ear to ear and trembling so hard that he had to sit down at the kitchen table.

He looked up at Simon and said, "Go get Ben, I have something exciting to tell you both."

Simon went into the other room to get Ben, wondering what news their dad had to tell them. When Simon had collected Ben from the living room, saying their dad had something to tell them both, they all gathered in the kitchen. Simon had had to promise Ben he could bring one of his new toys in with him just to get him into the other room.

Their dad placed an envelope on the table and said, "I bet you can't guess what this is?"

Simon didn't have a clue, and didn't want to guess because it really did seem that anything was possible this Christmas. For all Simon knew, it was the winning lottery ticket or something!

His dad spoke slowly, choosing his words carefully, "You won't believe it, but that was a messenger from your mum's office."

Ben sat up and beamed, "Is Mummy coming back to us?"

He smiled, a little sadness behind the smile, but shook his head saying, "No, Ben, she won't be coming home any time soon." He then looked at Simon and hinted, "Simon, this is even better than her coming back to us."

Simon looked up from Ben's new toy he had been studying and asked, "Better? I wonder... Has the magic of Christmas melted Scrooge's heart, and she's sent us some money to help out after leaving us in the lurch?"

Their dad's eyes lit up and he laughed, "Yes!" He then tore open the envelope and with tear filled eyes said, "It's a check for three million pounds! She's written to say she's living in Spain now, won the lottery, and felt it was only right to send us one million each! Each, Simon! You can quit your job and focus on your schoolwork again, son."

Ben's eyes were as big as saucepans he was that excited, and started singing, "We're rich, we're rich, and Mummy is a witch!"

Simon leaned over to his dad and hugged him, whispering, "The magic of Christmas has performed a miracle."

It was then Simon heard Santa's jolly laugh, as his last words echoed inside his head "Remember the Magic!"

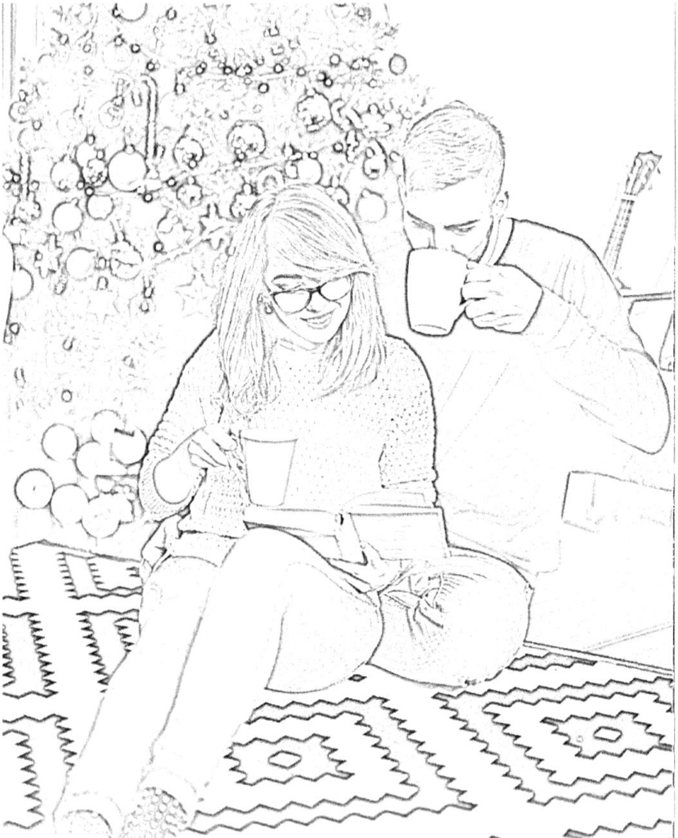

Epilogue...

She stood on the water's edge with the sea lapping at her toes. The cold water was keeping her centred on the ground ebbing and flowing beneath her feet, while her glazed eyes stared straight ahead.

Looking out to sea, as the breeze picked up, her brown locks danced in the air, and her eyes began to water slightly. And yet she did not flinch. She no longer felt the chill of the icy air biting at her bare shoulders.

The party had ended hours ago, and yet she remained. She alone had stayed to watch this moment.

She stood on that beach, looking out to sea, and thinking about all the other people who had stood there too. They might have been standing in the same spot in their time, but it would never be the same beach again.

Never the same bit of sand, nor would it be the same bit of water ever again either. But, as she stood there, she thought of all the people who had been in her position and done exactly what she was doing.

She wondered what they had thought about. What they had seen. And where they were now, as a new dawn was rising to greet her.

She looked out to where the sea met the sky, and the world appeared to end, knowing that there was a beautiful new beginning just out of sight. If she could hold on. If she could wait just a few more minutes. The new beginning would be hers for the taking. All she had to do was be patient and stay a few more minutes. Seconds, even. The world around her seemed to be holding its breath, waiting and wishing.

As the sky began to lighten before her eyes, and the lemon light pushed the darkness back to allow the burning orange that followed, she stared as long as she could at the white circle of the sun slowly rising from the water's edge.

Her eyes closed against the brightness, and she sighed with relief. Here she stood, on the cusp of a new beginning. A new beginning filled with hope. One filled with love and laughter and kindness. One that was anyone's for the taking, but she would be the first. Family, friends, strangers she was yet to meet but might never be able to imagine life without afterwards.

She thought not of the hurt, the anger, the grief or the hardships. Instead, she made herself think of all the possibilities. All the what ifs and maybes. Anything seemed possible in that moment.

She was breathing in time with the water lapping at her toes, the cold water still reminding her she was alive, and how beautiful a gift that is.

When the rays of light and warmth hit her face, she turned her head towards the heavens and let the air in her lungs soar out to meet the candyfloss clouds above her head. A seagull let out a cry, circling in the distance, breaking the silence of her sanctuary.

With a gentle smile, she closed her eyes again, breathed in the smell of the coastal air, and to the new day whispered, "Happy New Year."

Acknowledgments

Firstly, my thanks must go to my family, without whom I would never have had the time, patience, or courage to write. From a young age encouraging reading, writing, and anything creative, you have created a world in which it's okay to try new things, and you've supported me when they haven't always gone to plan. Thank you all.

To my parents for teaching me to love Christmas, and for making each one special for its own reasons. Without you two, the magic of Christmas would never have existed as it does. Thank you for your patience and understanding, and for answering my numerous questions while I wrote.

To Rachel, for making each Christmas Day as fun and exciting as you can. For your support and love that only a sister could give. For pushing me always to be a better person, so I could think myself worthy of your love and support. And for putting up with me acting like the child around this time of year. This Christmas simply won't be the same without you in the same house – insisting on watching It's A

Wonderful life on Christmas Eve, refusing to go to sleep even though you're exhausted, and waking up early to open your presents. I hope your first Christmas as a newly qualified midwife is a good one, and I can't wait to see you as soon as you can.

To Cameron, for being the one to suggest a compilation. This book wouldn't have come about without you. What may have seemed a flippant comment over lunch one Friday, was the catalyst to finally sitting myself down and working.

Thank you to Kayleigh. Without your help and support, I'm not sure I would have survived the late night writing sessions, or the exhaustion of the next day. Also, a big thank you for your help in deciding on a front cover. The excitement of seeing it come to life wouldn't have been as high without your input.

Vada and Francesca. You two made me believe it was possible to love Christmas and not be judged for that, even when thinking about the festive period mid-summer when everyone else dreams of their summer sun. Even with the year being tough, you two have been a ray of sunshine despite your own circumstances, and your friendship and support has meant the world to me.

A special thanks to Ray. Though you may never read this, your guide to self-publishing was my motivation to keep going. Without it, I would never have reached this stage.

And finally, thank you to you – the reader. It has been a tough year for many of us. While Christmas is usually a time filled with joy, laughter, friends and family, this one is different for many of us. Thank you for taking the time to read my writings, and for welcoming the Christmas spirit into your lives.

About the Author

Katie was born and brought up between Forfar, Scotland and Lisburn, Northern Ireland, where she lives with her parents and their cat, Maisey. Having fallen in love with reading and writing at a young age, Katie was rarely found without a book in hand and often took one into school for when she finished the classwork early. Taking pride in having poetry published twice by the Foyle Young Poets of the Year, Katie soon turned her attention from poetry and song lyrics to writing short stories and plays for her friends to perform in front of their parents.

After years of dabbling with fictional work, Katie started her lifestyle blog as an outlet for her creative writing while at university. Before long, her blog became Christmas orientated for the majority of the year, and it was during the lockdown of 2020 that she finally put pen to paper to write her first collection of Christmas short stories when she wasn't struggling to learn guitar.

You can say hello to Katie on

Twitter @kvburton657

Facebook @ Life With Ktkinnes Blog

www.lifewithktkinnes.com

www.christmaswithkatie.com

Printed in Great Britain
by Amazon